W9-ATT-642

@ Your Library

Summer Reading 2009

This book is in honor of

Yasmin Rincon

for outstanding reading.

Lucy Robbins Welles
LIBRARY

95 Cedar Street, Newington, CT 06111-2645
Children's: 860-665-8720 FAX: 860-667-1255
http://www.newingtonct.gov/library

Kat & Mouse™
2 tripped

Story by Alex de Campi
Art by Federica Manfredi

LUCY ROBBINS WELLES LIBRARY
95 CEDAR STREET
NEWINGTON, CT 06111

TOKYOPOP®

HAMBURG // LONDON // LOS ANGELES // TOKYO

Spotlight

visit us at www.abdopublishing.com

Reinforced library bound edition published in 2009 by Spotlight, a division of ABDO Publishing Group, 8000 West 78th Street, Edina, Minnesota 55439. This edition reprinted by arrangement with TOKYOPOP Inc. www.tokyopop.com

© 2006 Alex de Campi and TOKYOPOP Inc. "Kat & Mouse" is a trademark of TOKYOPOP Inc.

All rights reserved. No part of this book may be reproduced or transmitted in any form or by any means without written permission from the copyright holder. This book is a work of fiction. Any resemblance to actual events or locales or persons, living or dead, is entirely coincidental.

Written by	Alex de Campi
Illustrated by	Federica Manfredi
Tones	Christine Schilling
Lettering	Lucas Rivera
Cover Design	Jose Macasocol Jr. & Federica Manfredi
Editors	Tim Beedle & Carol Fox
Digital Imaging Manager	Chris Buford

Library of Congress Cataloging-in-Publication Data

De Campi, Alex.

Kat & Mouse / story by Alex de Campi ; art by Federica Manfredi. -- Reinforced library bound ed.

v. cm.

Summary: Collects three previously published manga volumes in which classmates Kat Foster and Mee-Seen "Mouse" Huang investigate events involving their private school, Dover Academy, and a mysterious thief known as the Artful Dodger.

Contents: Teacher torture -- Tripped -- The ice storm.

ISBN 978-1-59961-565-3 (vol. 2: Tripped : alk. paper)

1. Graphic novels. [1. Graphic novels. 2. Schools--Fiction. 3. Friendship--Fiction. 4. Robbers and outlaws--Fiction. 5. Mystery and detective stories.] I. Manfredi, Federica, ill. II. Title. III. Title: Kat and Mouse.

PZ7.7.D32Kat 2009

[Fic]--dc22   2008002189

All Spotlight books have reinforced library binding and are manufactured in the United States of America.

Kat & Mouse

TABLE OF CONTENTS

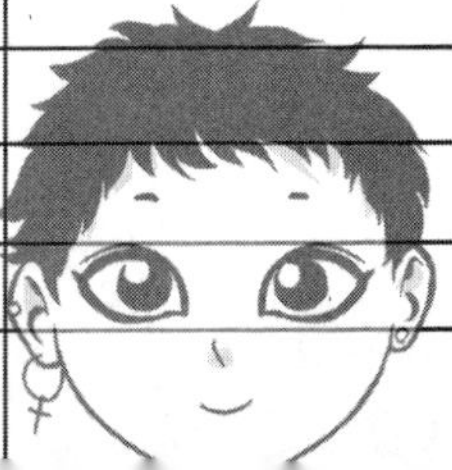

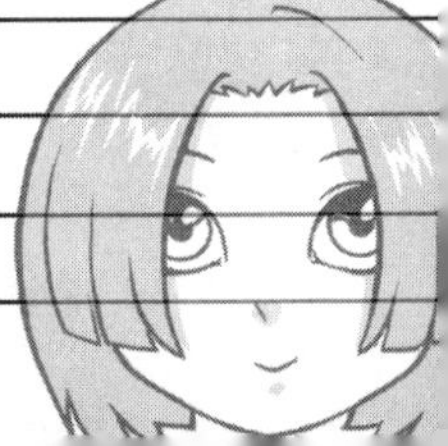

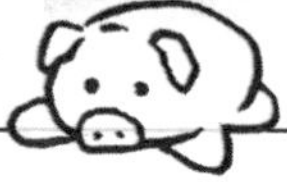

PREVIOUSLY...

Kat Foster would have been happy finishing off her seventh grade year in her hometown in Iowa. But when her father accepts a new job teaching science at a prestigious private school in New Hampshire, she has no choice but to pack up her things and move with her family to Dover—a wealthy community where they don't exactly fit in. Kat stands out at her new school, and quickly falls to the bottom of the social ladder, but she does make one new friend: Mee-Seen Huang. Mee-Seen—or "Mouse" as she prefers to be known—is a punky skateboarder who also has trouble fitting in at Dover Academy...and that's just the way she likes it.

Together, Kat and Mouse face many challenges, most of which are caused by The Artful Dodger—a mysterious thief who has been stealing valuables at their school. Kat and Mouse have vowed to bring the thief to justice. However, despite their best efforts, the identity of The Artful Dodger remains a mystery.

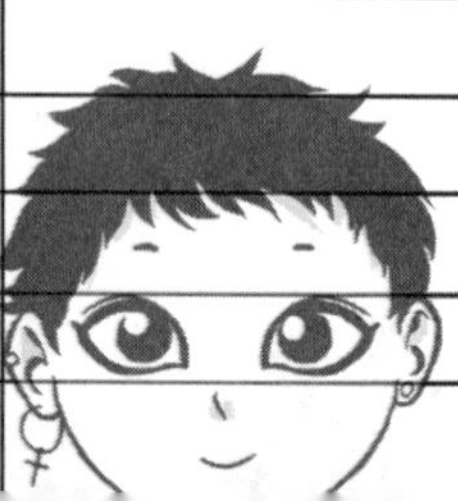

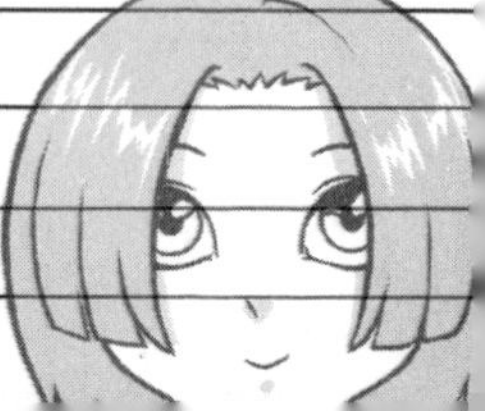

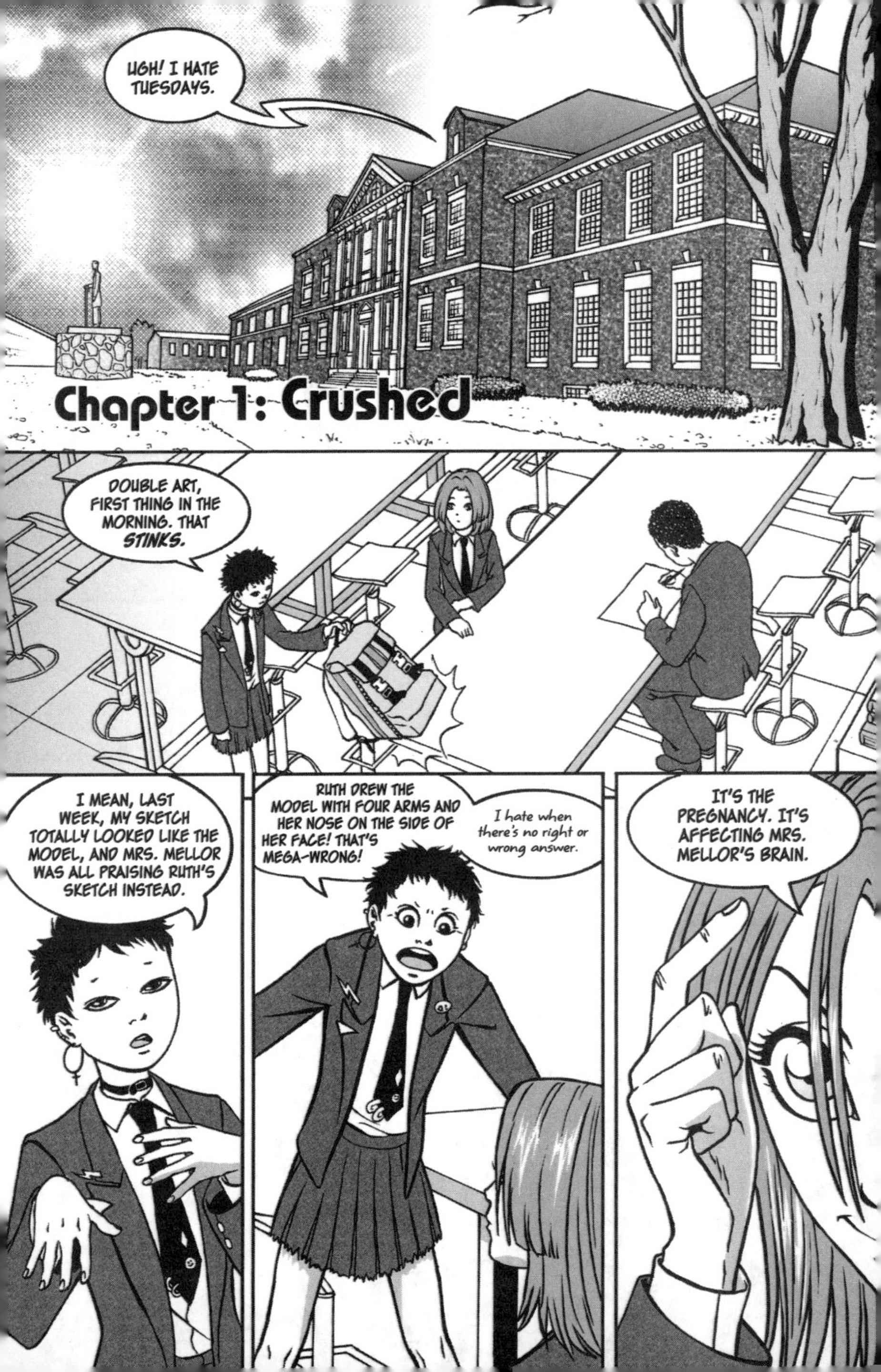

UGH! I HATE TUESDAYS.
Chapter 1: Crushed
DOUBLE ART, FIRST THING IN THE MORNING. THAT STINKS.
I MEAN, LAST WEEK, MY SKETCH TOTALLY LOOKED LIKE THE MODEL, AND MRS. MELLOR WAS ALL PRAISING RUTH'S SKETCH INSTEAD.
RUTH DREW THE MODEL WITH FOUR ARMS AND HER NOSE ON THE SIDE OF HER FACE! THAT'S MEGA-WRONG!
I hate when there's no right or wrong answer.
IT'S THE PREGNANCY. IT'S AFFECTING MRS. MELLOR'S BRAIN.

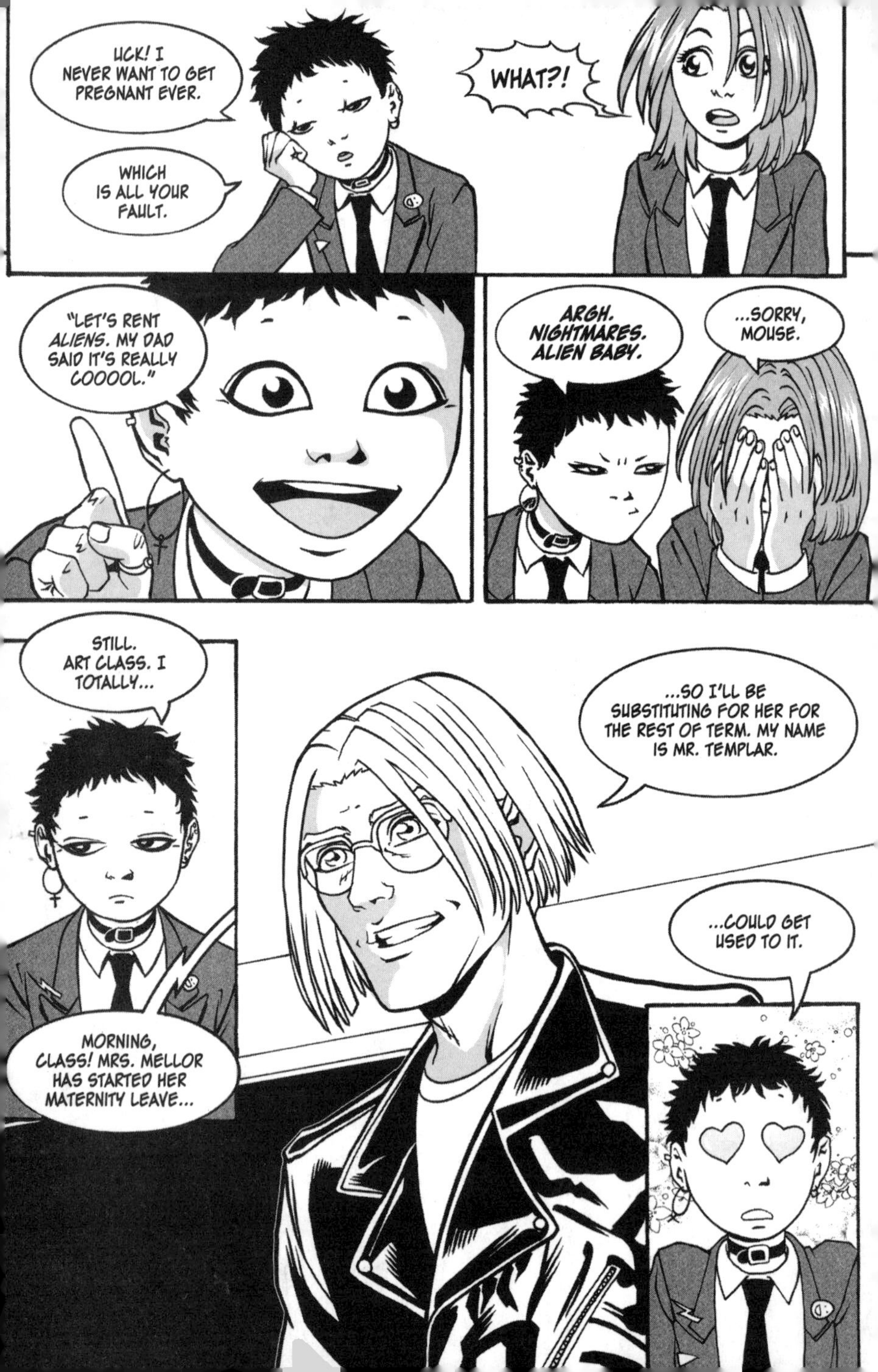
UCK! I NEVER WANT TO GET PREGNANT EVER.
WHICH IS ALL YOUR FAULT.
WHAT?!
"LET'S RENT ALIENS. MY DAD SAID IT'S REALLY COOOOL."
ARGH. NIGHTMARES. ALIEN BABY.
...SORRY, MOUSE.
STILL. ART CLASS. I TOTALLY...
MORNING, CLASS! MRS. MELLOR HAS STARTED HER MATERNITY LEAVE...
...SO I'LL BE SUBSTITUTING FOR HER FOR THE REST OF TERM. MY NAME IS MR. TEMPLAR.
...COULD GET USED TO IT.

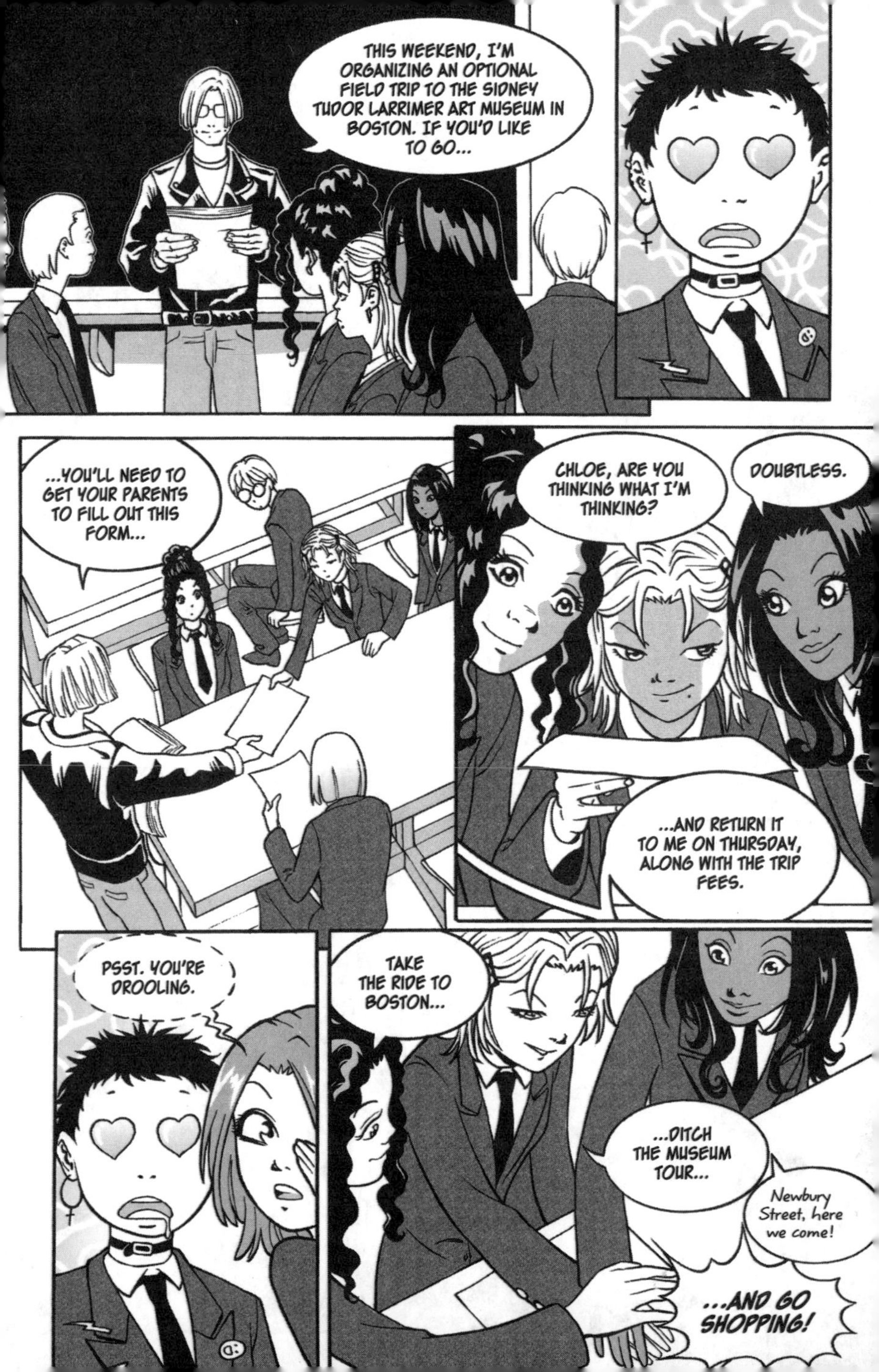
THIS WEEKEND, I'M ORGANIZING AN OPTIONAL FIELD TRIP TO THE SIDNEY TUDOR LARRIMER ART MUSEUM IN BOSTON. IF YOU'D LIKE TO GO...
...YOU'LL NEED TO GET YOUR PARENTS TO FILL OUT THIS FORM...
CHLOE, ARE YOU THINKING WHAT I'M THINKING?
DOUBTLESS.
...AND RETURN IT TO ME ON THURSDAY, ALONG WITH THE TRIP FEES.
PSST. YOU'RE DROOLING.
TAKE THE RIDE TO BOSTON...
...DITCH THE MUSEUM TOUR...
Newbury Street, here we come!
...AND GO SHOPPING!

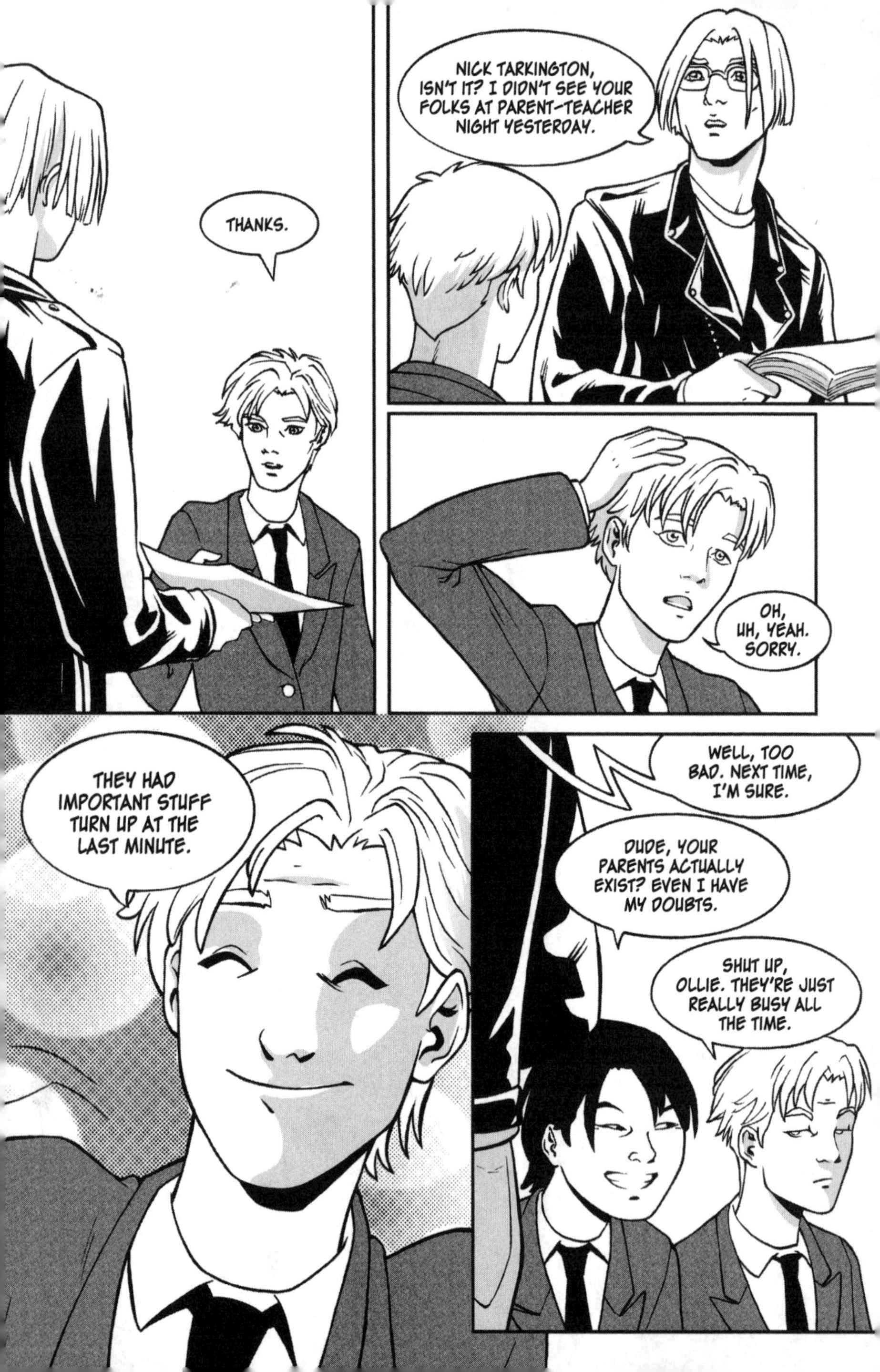
THANKS.
NICK TARKINGTON, ISN'T IT? I DIDN'T SEE YOUR FOLKS AT PARENT-TEACHER NIGHT YESTERDAY.
OH, UH, YEAH. SORRY.
THEY HAD IMPORTANT STUFF TURN UP AT THE LAST MINUTE.
WELL, TOO BAD. NEXT TIME, I'M SURE.
DUDE, YOUR PARENTS ACTUALLY EXIST? EVEN I HAVE MY DOUBTS.
SHUT UP, OLLIE. THEY'RE JUST REALLY BUSY ALL THE TIME.

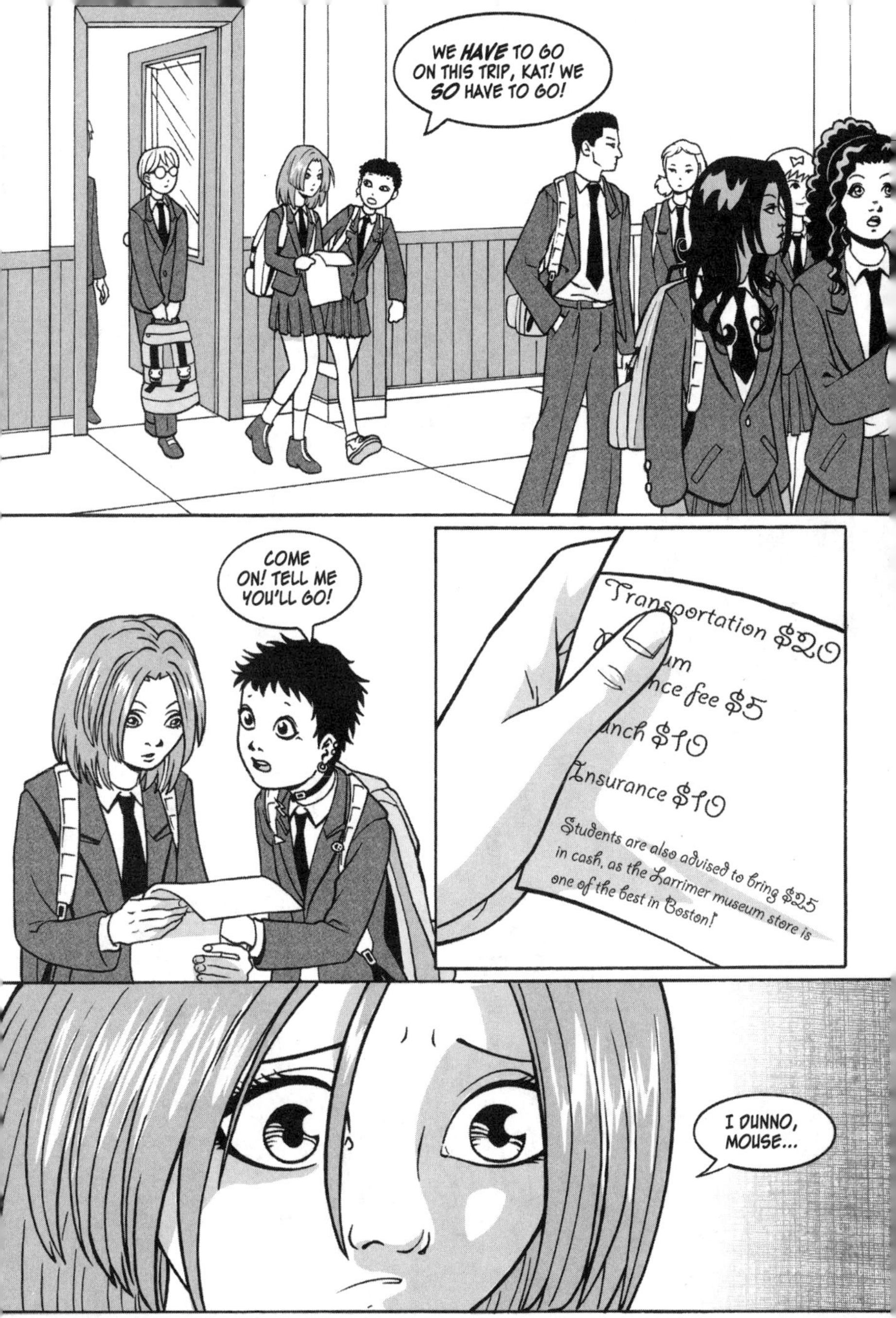
WE HAVE TO GO ON THIS TRIP, KAT! WE SO HAVE TO GO!
COME ON! TELL ME YOU'LL GO!
Transportation $20
um
nce fee $5
unch $10
Insurance $10
Students are also advised to bring $25 in cash, as the Larrimer museum store is one of the best in Boston!
I DUNNO, MOUSE...

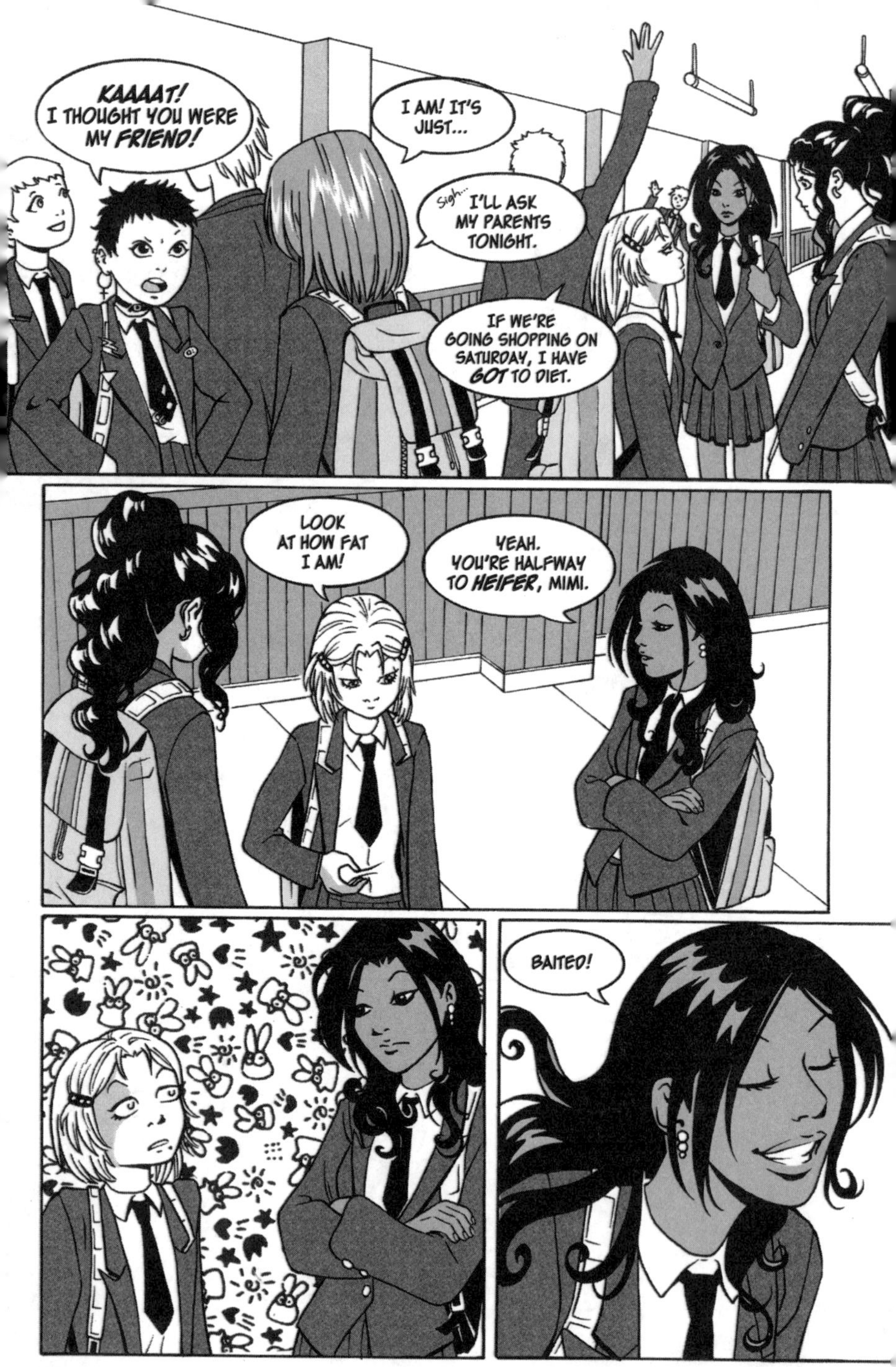
KAAAAT! I THOUGHT YOU WERE MY FRIEND!
I AM! IT'S JUST...
Sigh... I'LL ASK MY PARENTS TONIGHT.
IF WE'RE GOING SHOPPING ON SATURDAY, I HAVE GOT TO DIET.
LOOK AT HOW FAT I AM!
YEAH. YOU'RE HALFWAY TO HEIFER, MIMI.
BAITED!

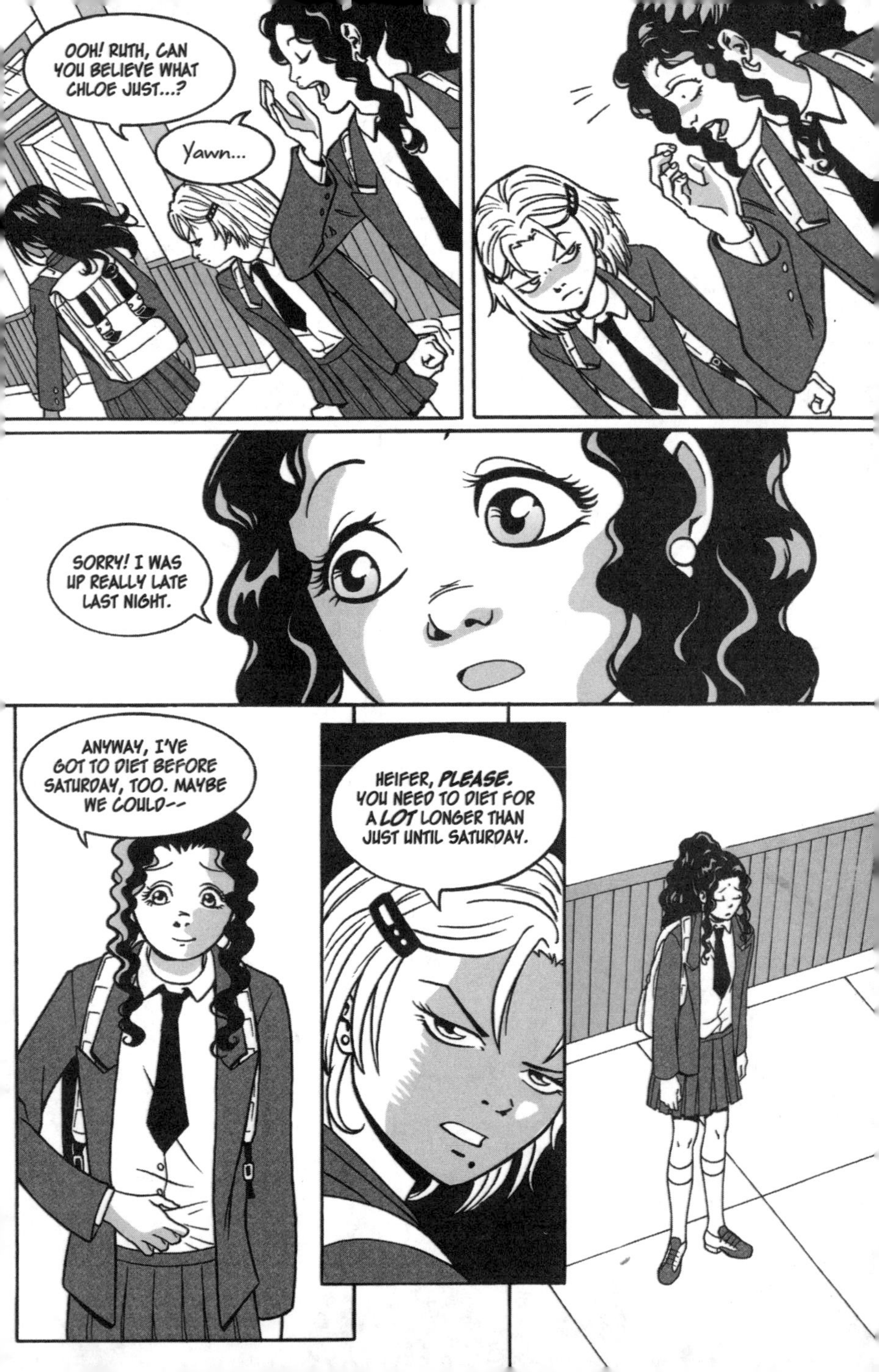
OOH! RUTH, CAN YOU BELIEVE WHAT CHLOE JUST...?
Yawn...
SORRY! I WAS UP REALLY LATE LAST NIGHT.
ANYWAY, I'VE GOT TO DIET BEFORE SATURDAY, TOO. MAYBE WE COULD--
HEIFER, PLEASE. YOU NEED TO DIET FOR A LOT LONGER THAN JUST UNTIL SATURDAY.

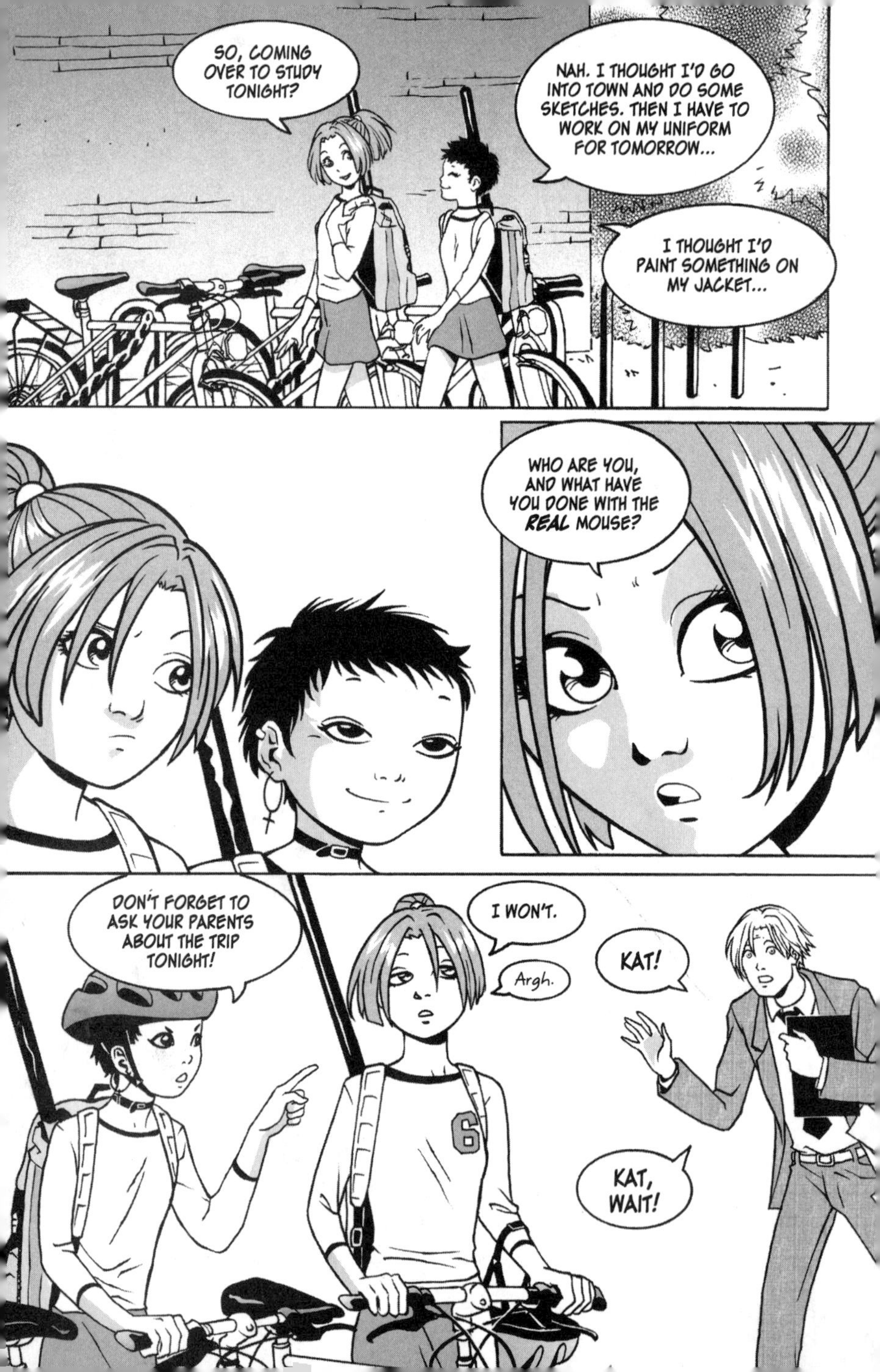
SO, COMING OVER TO STUDY TONIGHT?
NAH. I THOUGHT I'D GO INTO TOWN AND DO SOME SKETCHES. THEN I HAVE TO WORK ON MY UNIFORM FOR TOMORROW...
I THOUGHT I'D PAINT SOMETHING ON MY JACKET...
WHO ARE YOU, AND WHAT HAVE YOU DONE WITH THE *REAL* MOUSE?
DON'T FORGET TO ASK YOUR PARENTS ABOUT THE TRIP TONIGHT!
I WON'T.
Argh.
KAT!
KAT, WAIT!

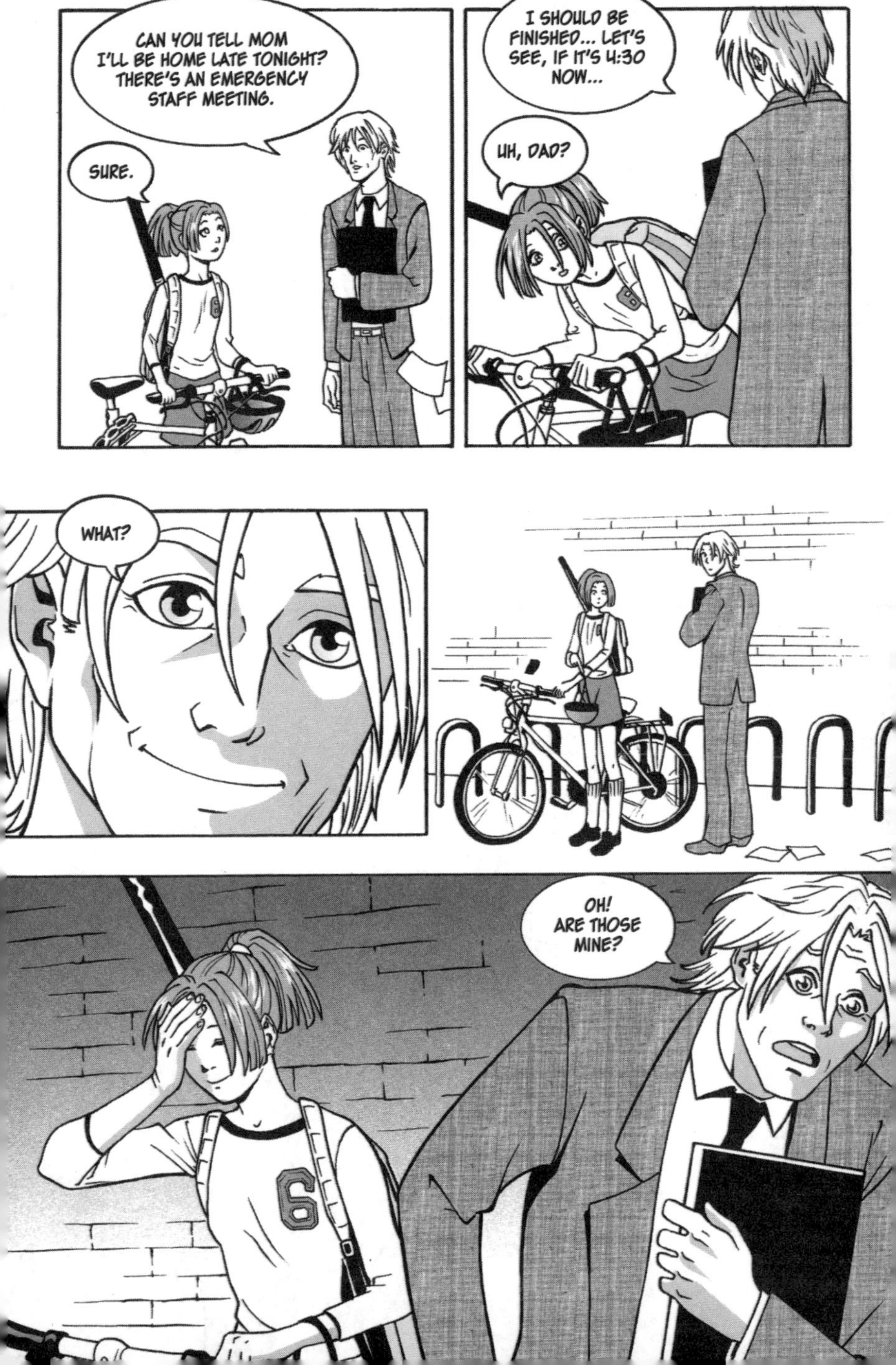
CAN YOU TELL MOM I'LL BE HOME LATE TONIGHT? THERE'S AN EMERGENCY STAFF MEETING.
SURE.
I SHOULD BE FINISHED... LET'S SEE, IF IT'S 4:30 NOW...
UH, DAD?
WHAT?
OH! ARE THOSE MINE?

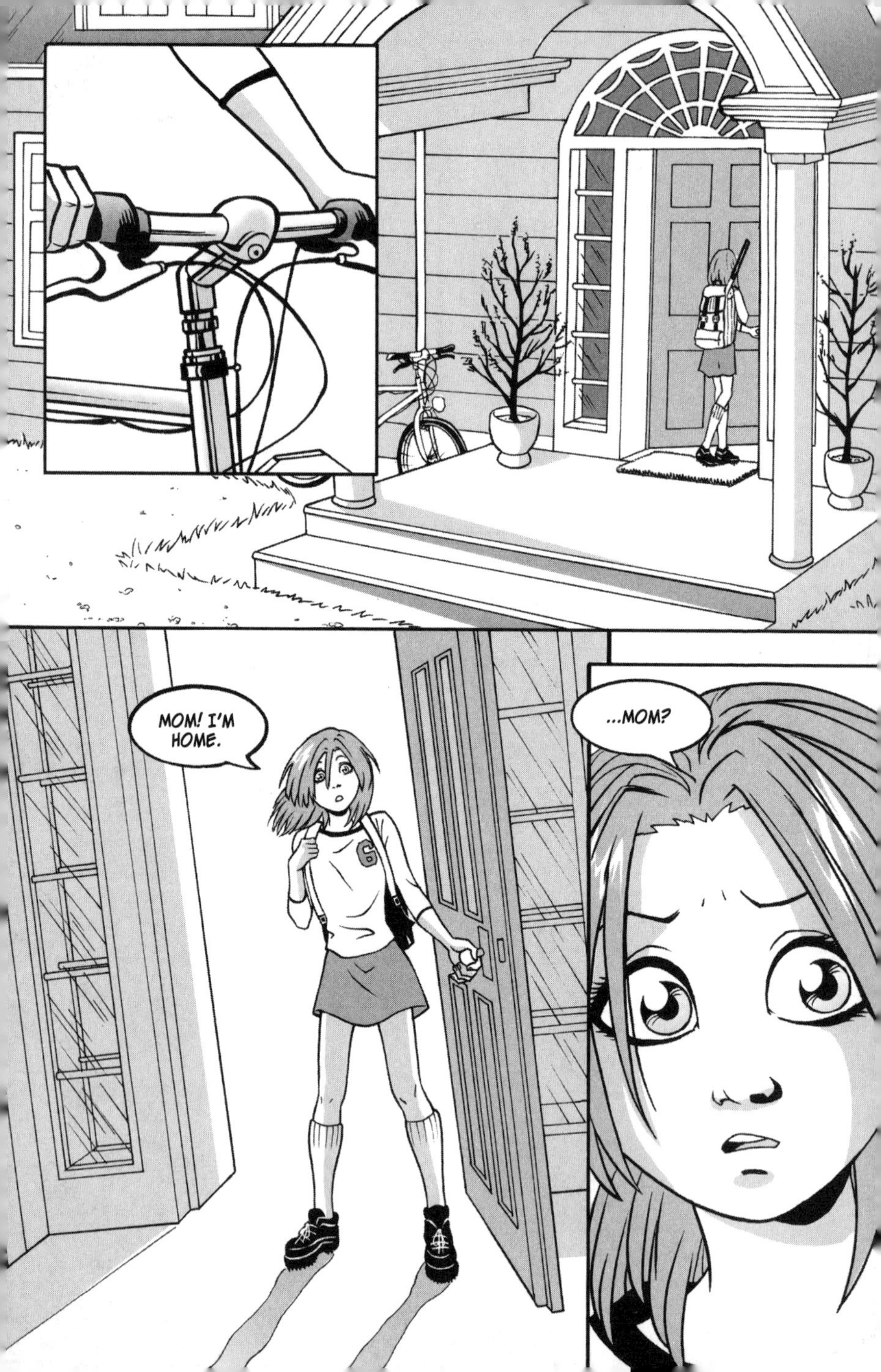
MOM! I'M HOME.
...MOM?

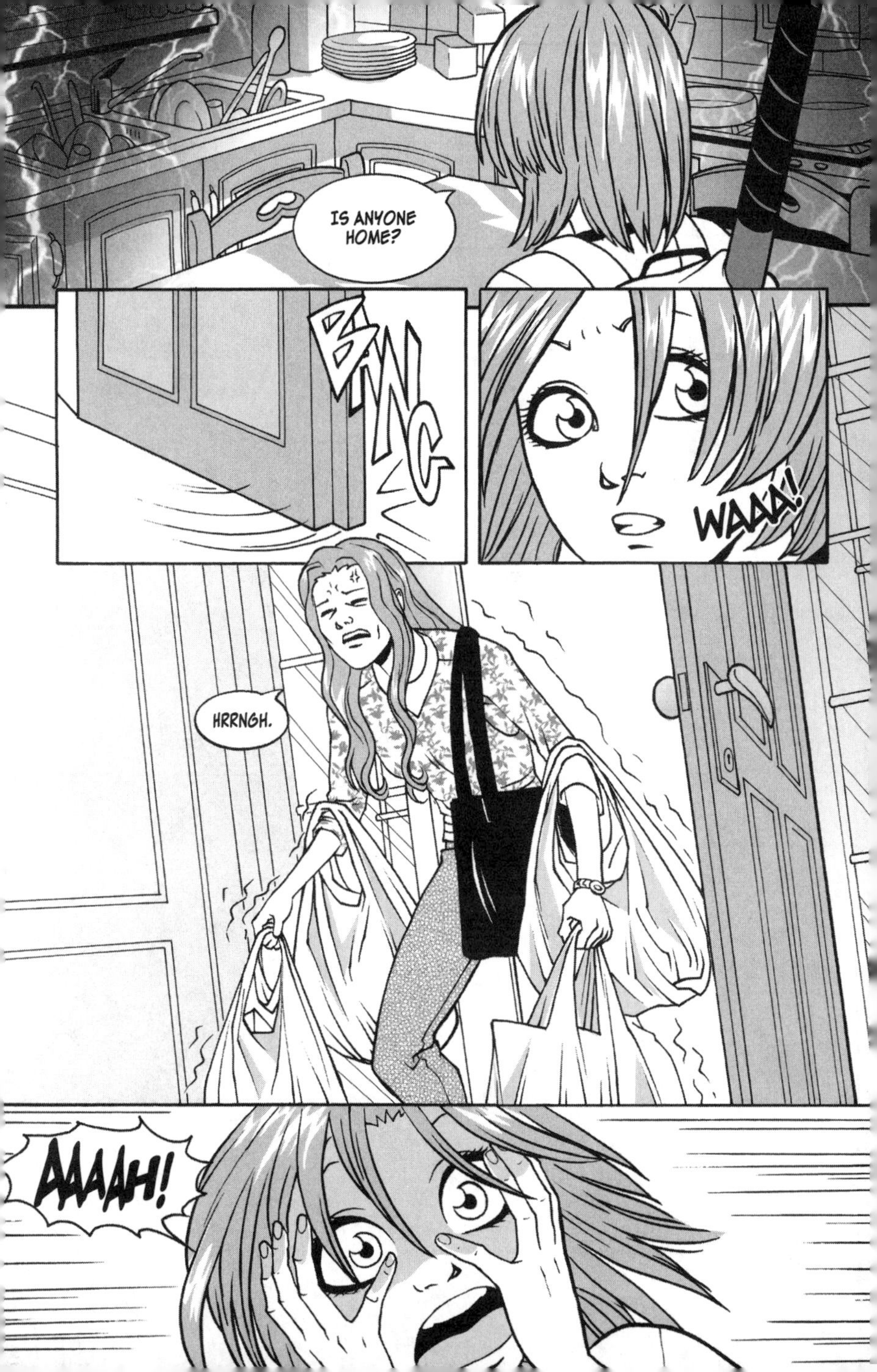
IS ANYONE HOME?
BANG
WAAA!
HRRNGH.
AAAAH!

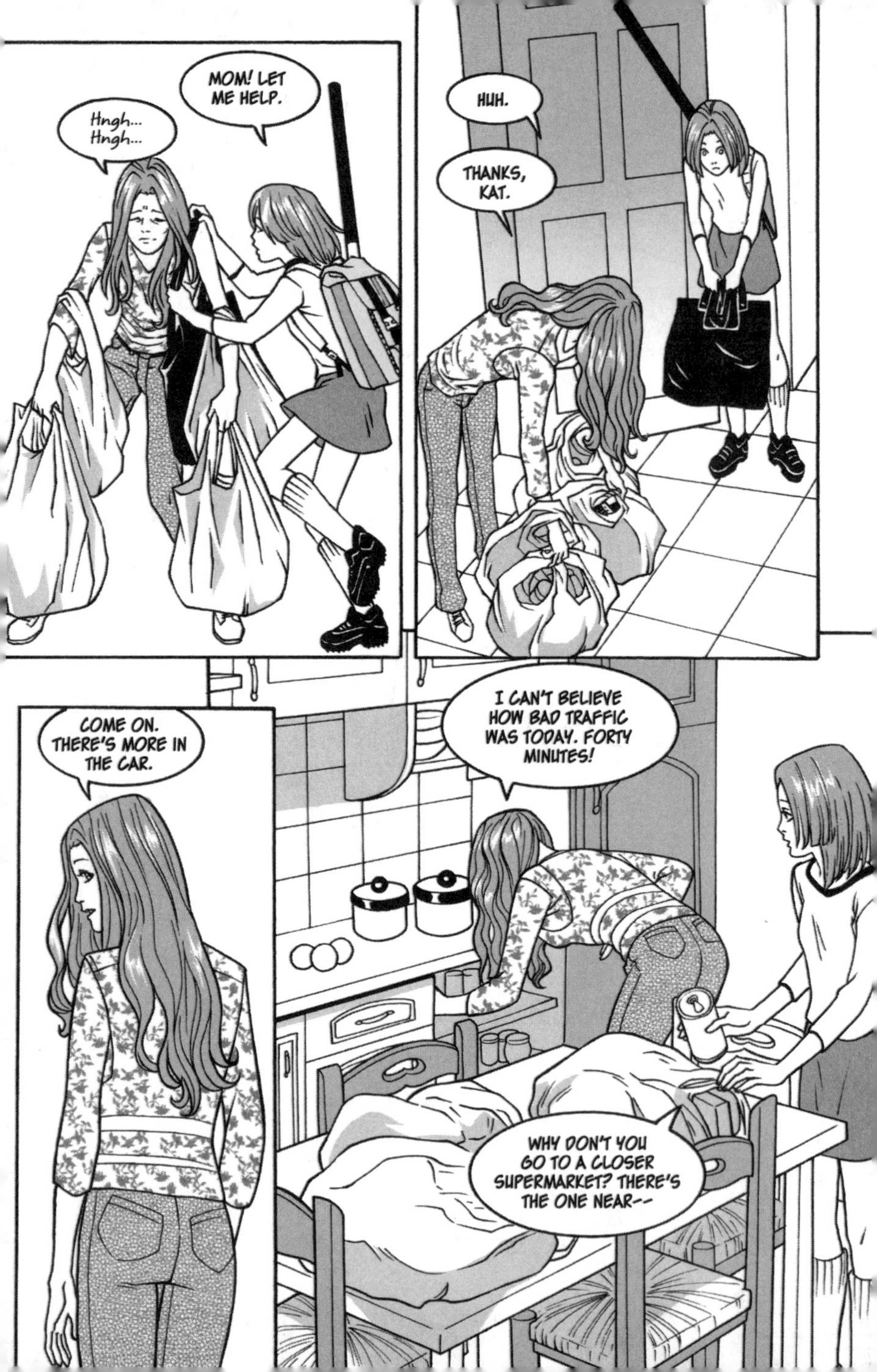
Hngh...
Hngh...
MOM! LET ME HELP.
HUH.
THANKS, KAT.
COME ON. THERE'S MORE IN THE CAR.
I CAN'T BELIEVE HOW BAD TRAFFIC WAS TODAY. FORTY MINUTES!
WHY DON'T YOU GO TO A CLOSER SUPERMARKET? THERE'S THE ONE NEAR--

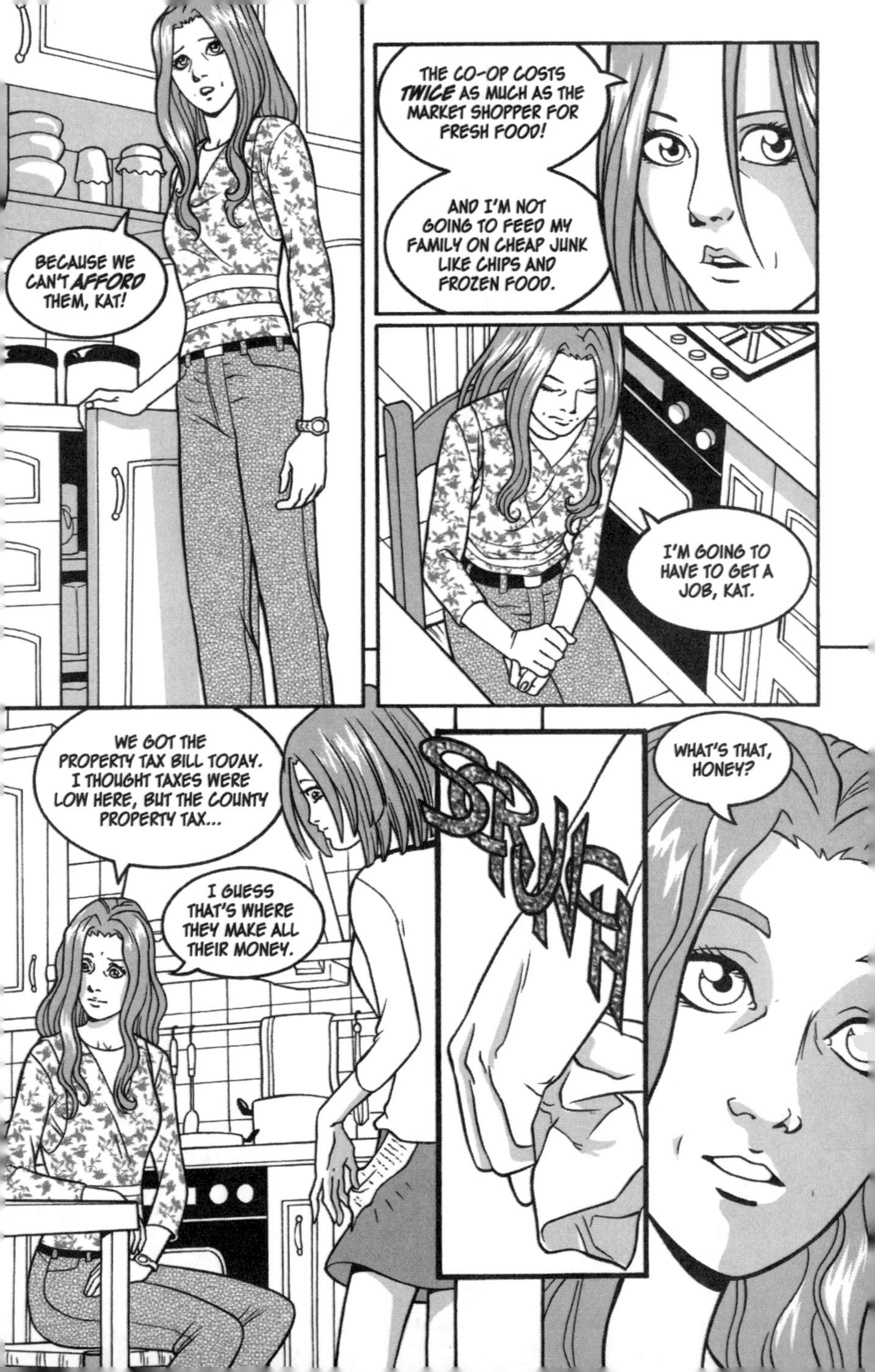
BECAUSE WE CAN'T AFFORD THEM, KAT!
THE CO-OP COSTS TWICE AS MUCH AS THE MARKET SHOPPER FOR FRESH FOOD!
AND I'M NOT GOING TO FEED MY FAMILY ON CHEAP JUNK LIKE CHIPS AND FROZEN FOOD.
I'M GOING TO HAVE TO GET A JOB, KAT.
WE GOT THE PROPERTY TAX BILL TODAY. I THOUGHT TAXES WERE LOW HERE, BUT THE COUNTY PROPERTY TAX...
I GUESS THAT'S WHERE THEY MAKE ALL THEIR MONEY.
SCRUNCH
WHAT'S THAT, HONEY?

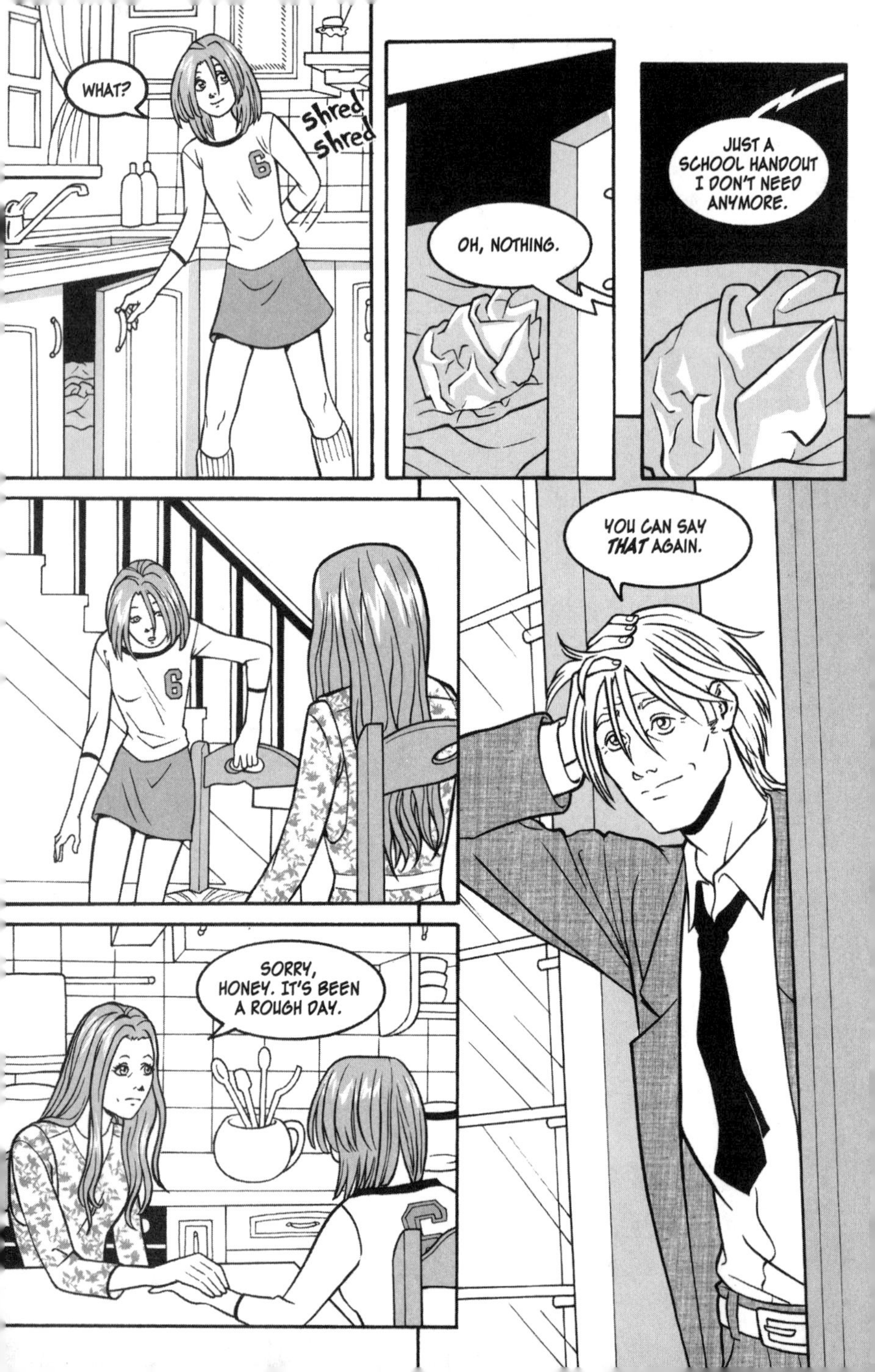
WHAT?
shred shred
OH, NOTHING.
JUST A SCHOOL HANDOUT I DON'T NEED ANYMORE.
YOU CAN SAY THAT AGAIN.
SORRY, HONEY. IT'S BEEN A ROUGH DAY.

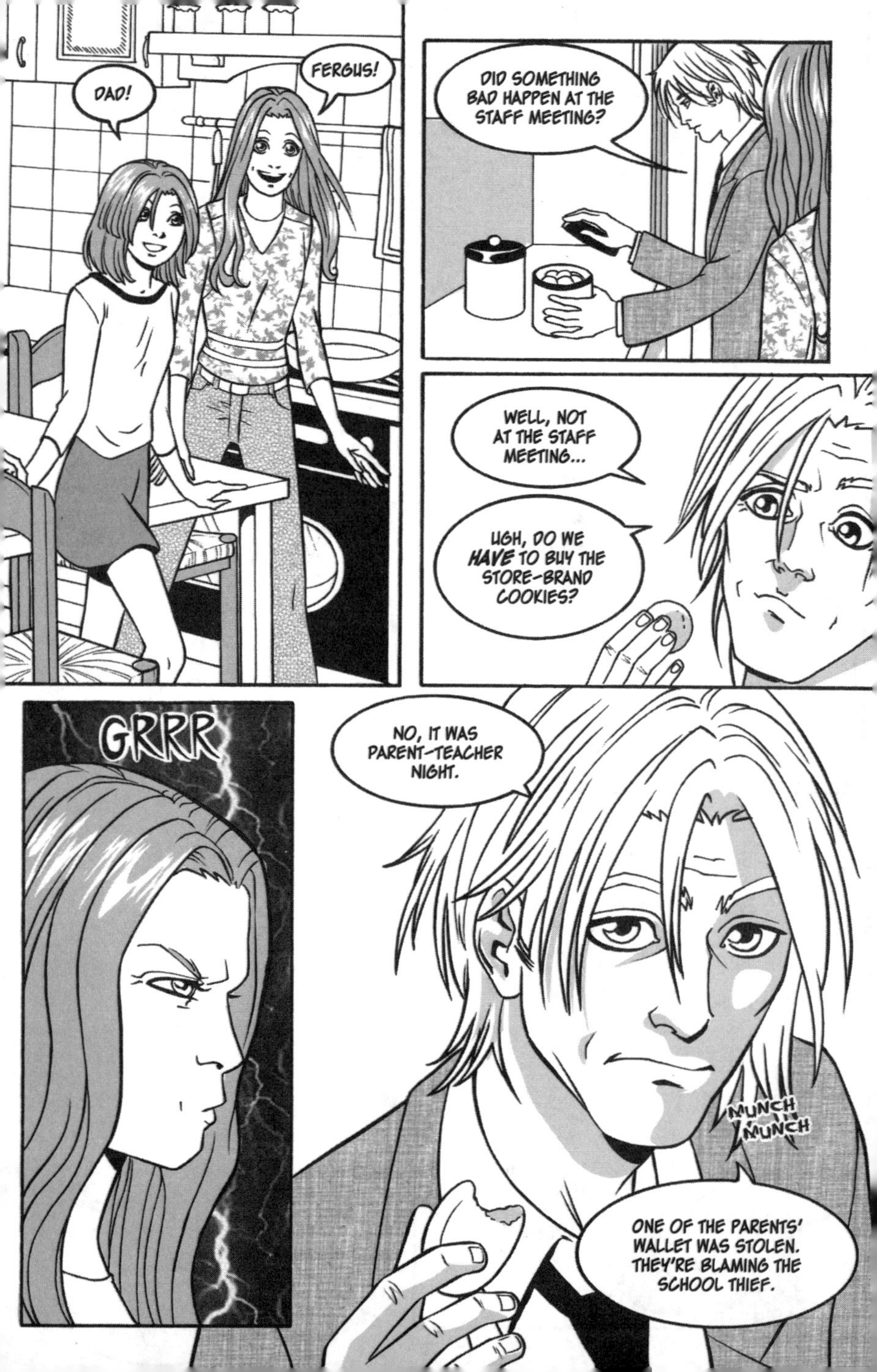

DAD!
FERGUS!
DID SOMETHING BAD HAPPEN AT THE STAFF MEETING?
WELL, NOT AT THE STAFF MEETING...
UGH, DO WE *HAVE* TO BUY THE STORE-BRAND COOKIES?
GRRR
NO, IT WAS PARENT-TEACHER NIGHT.
MUNCH MUNCH
ONE OF THE PARENTS' WALLET WAS STOLEN. THEY'RE BLAMING THE SCHOOL THIEF.

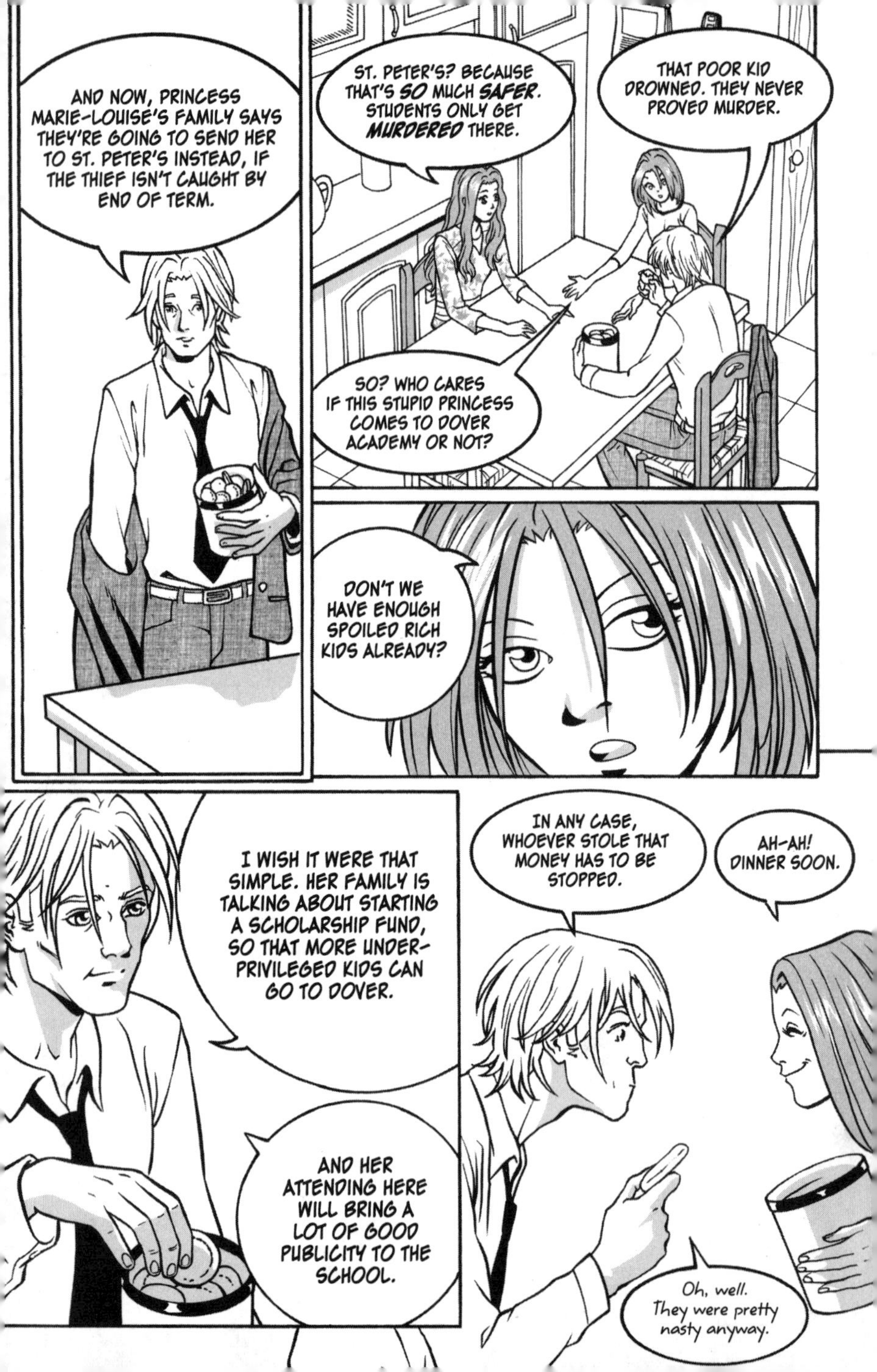
AND NOW, PRINCESS MARIE-LOUISE'S FAMILY SAYS THEY'RE GOING TO SEND HER TO ST. PETER'S INSTEAD, IF THE THIEF ISN'T CAUGHT BY END OF TERM.
ST. PETER'S? BECAUSE THAT'S SO MUCH SAFER. STUDENTS ONLY GET MURDERED THERE.
THAT POOR KID DROWNED. THEY NEVER PROVED MURDER.
SO? WHO CARES IF THIS STUPID PRINCESS COMES TO DOVER ACADEMY OR NOT?
DON'T WE HAVE ENOUGH SPOILED RICH KIDS ALREADY?
I WISH IT WERE THAT SIMPLE. HER FAMILY IS TALKING ABOUT STARTING A SCHOLARSHIP FUND, SO THAT MORE UNDER-PRIVILEGED KIDS CAN GO TO DOVER.
AND HER ATTENDING HERE WILL BRING A LOT OF GOOD PUBLICITY TO THE SCHOOL.
IN ANY CASE, WHOEVER STOLE THAT MONEY HAS TO BE STOPPED.
AH-AH! DINNER SOON.
Oh, well. They were pretty nasty anyway.

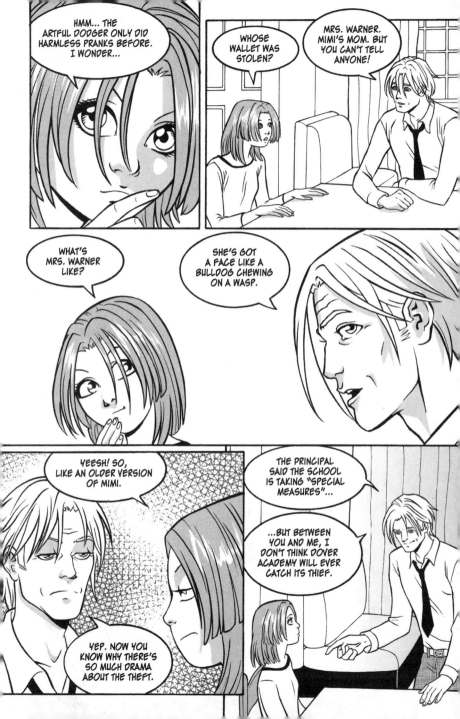

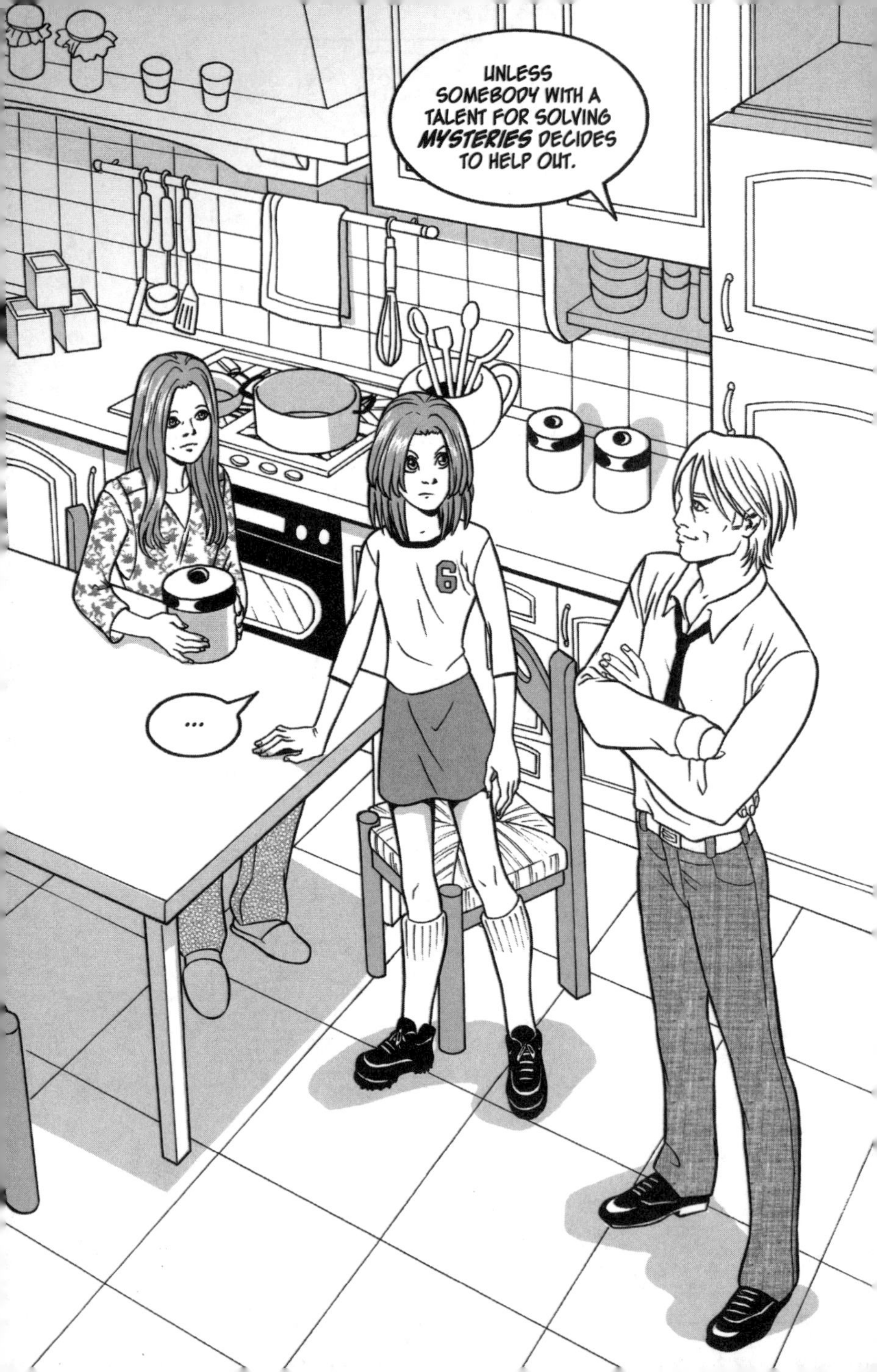
UNLESS SOMEBODY WITH A TALENT FOR SOLVING MYSTERIES DECIDES TO HELP OUT.
...

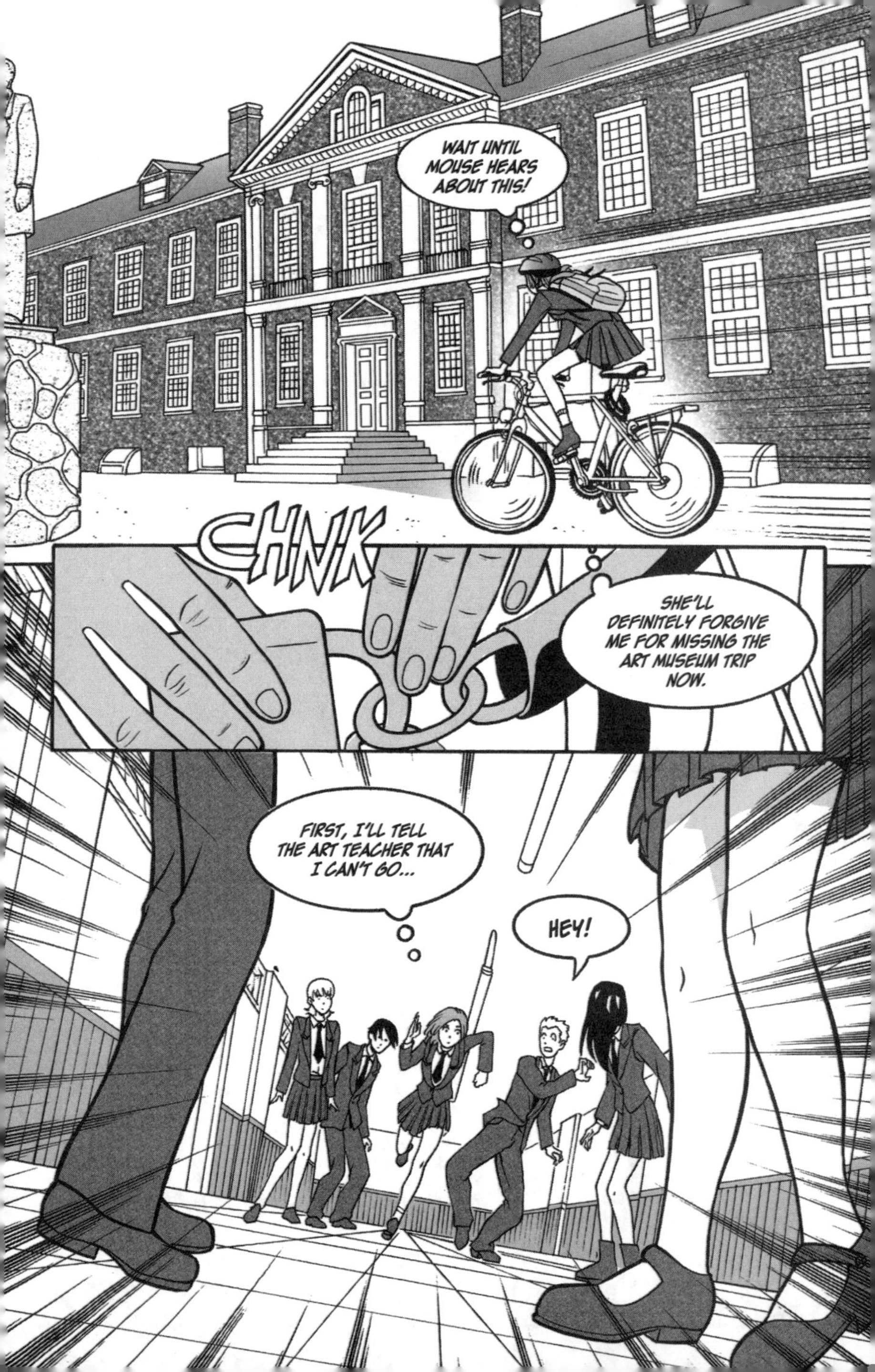
WAIT UNTIL MOUSE HEARS ABOUT THIS!
CHNK
SHE'LL DEFINITELY FORGIVE ME FOR MISSING THE ART MUSEUM TRIP NOW.
FIRST, I'LL TELL THE ART TEACHER THAT I CAN'T GO...
HEY!

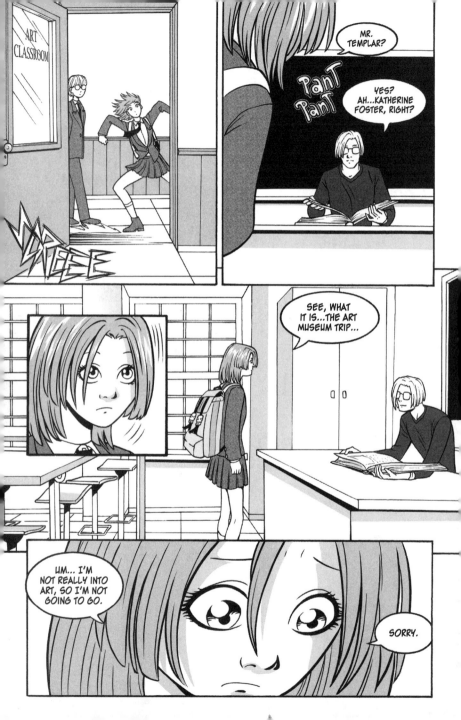

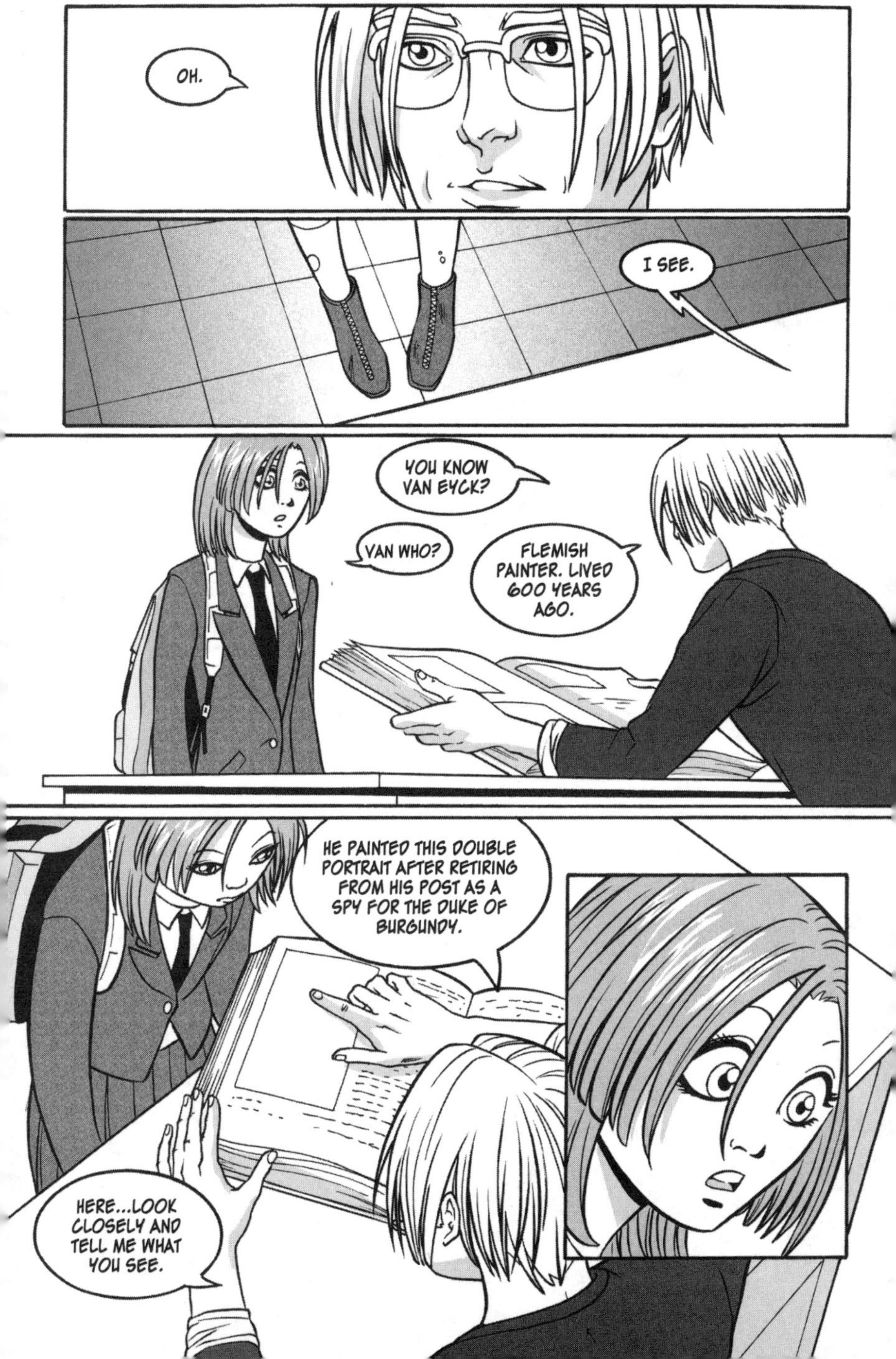
OH.
I SEE.
YOU KNOW VAN EYCK?
VAN WHO?
FLEMISH PAINTER. LIVED 600 YEARS AGO.
HE PAINTED THIS DOUBLE PORTRAIT AFTER RETIRING FROM HIS POST AS A SPY FOR THE DUKE OF BURGUNDY.
HERE...LOOK CLOSELY AND TELL ME WHAT YOU SEE.

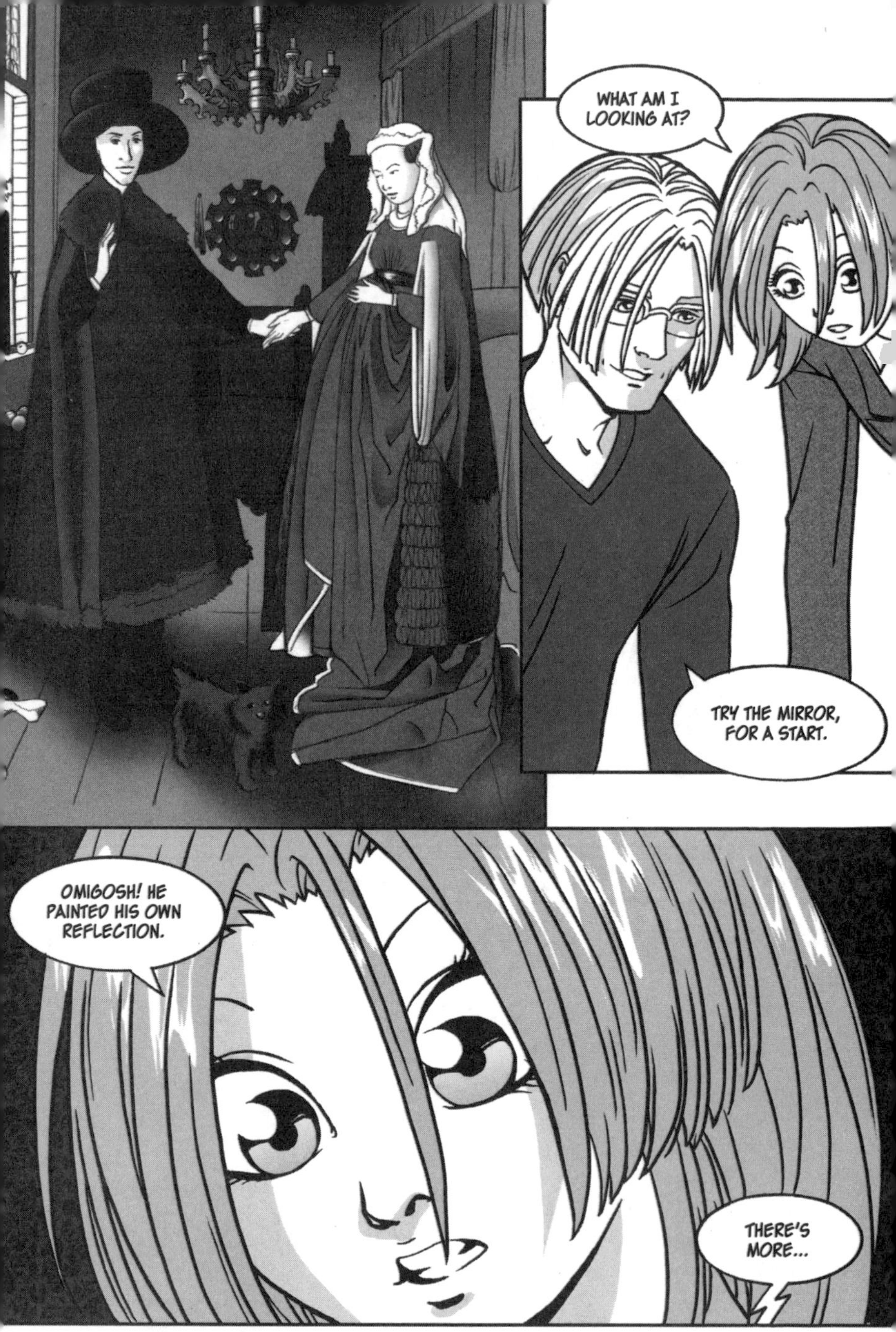
WHAT AM I LOOKING AT?
TRY THE MIRROR, FOR A START.
OMIGOSH! HE PAINTED HIS OWN REFLECTION.
THERE'S MORE...

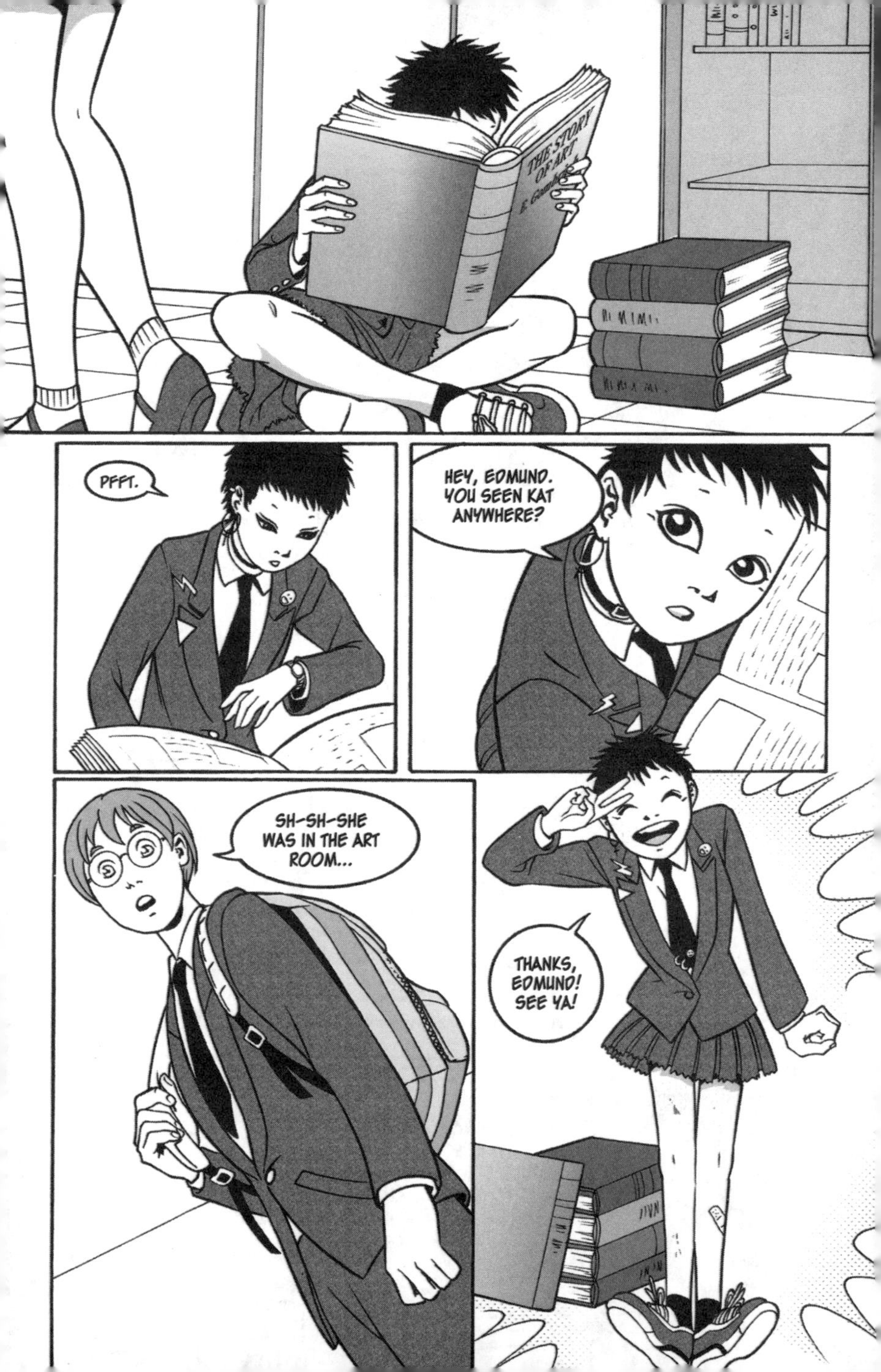
THE STORY OF ART
E. Gombrich
PFFT.
HEY, EDMUND. YOU SEEN KAT ANYWHERE?
SH-SH-SHE WAS IN THE ART ROOM...
THANKS, EDMUND! SEE YA!

Chapter 2:
The Worst Day Since Yesterday

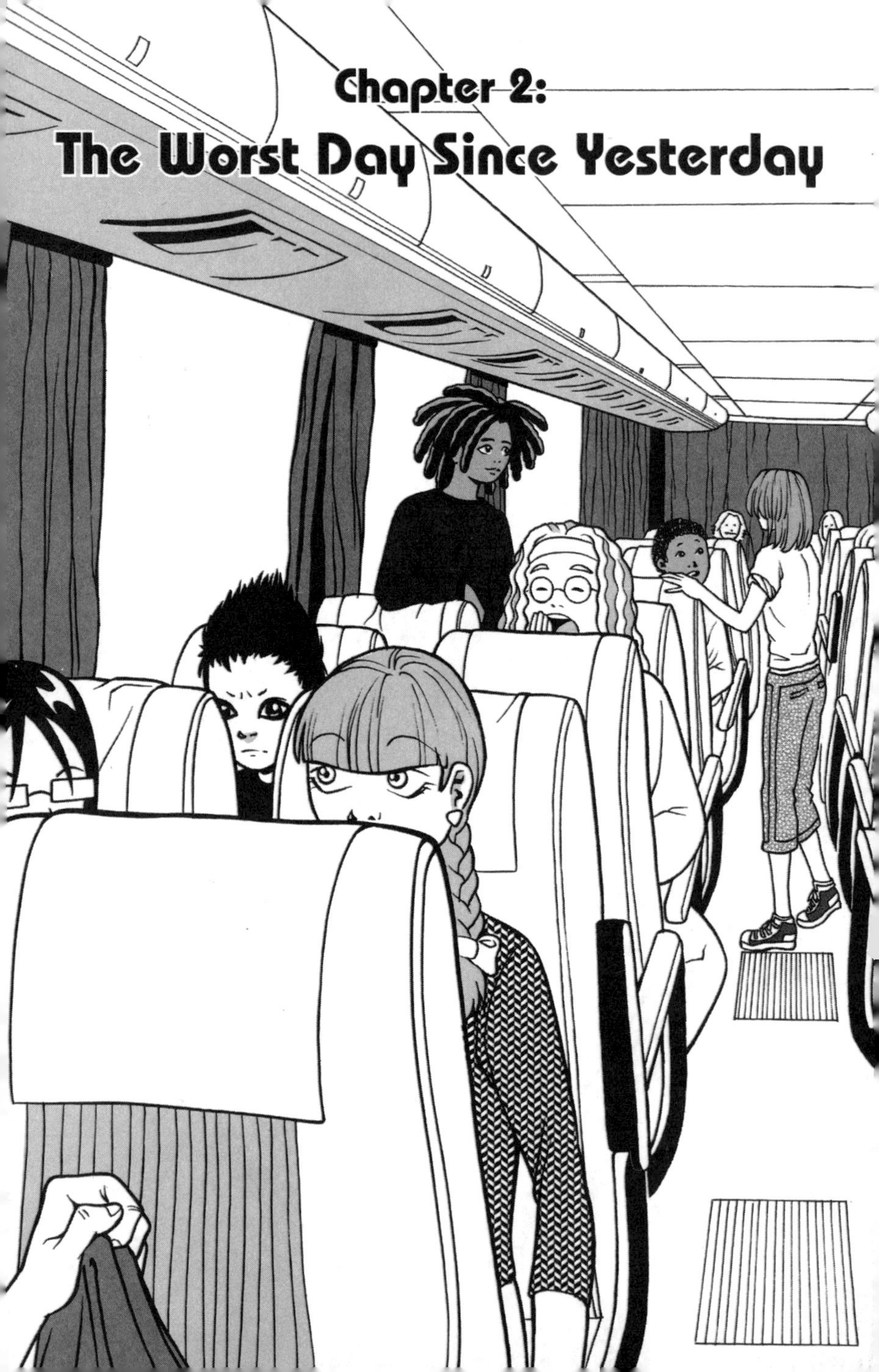

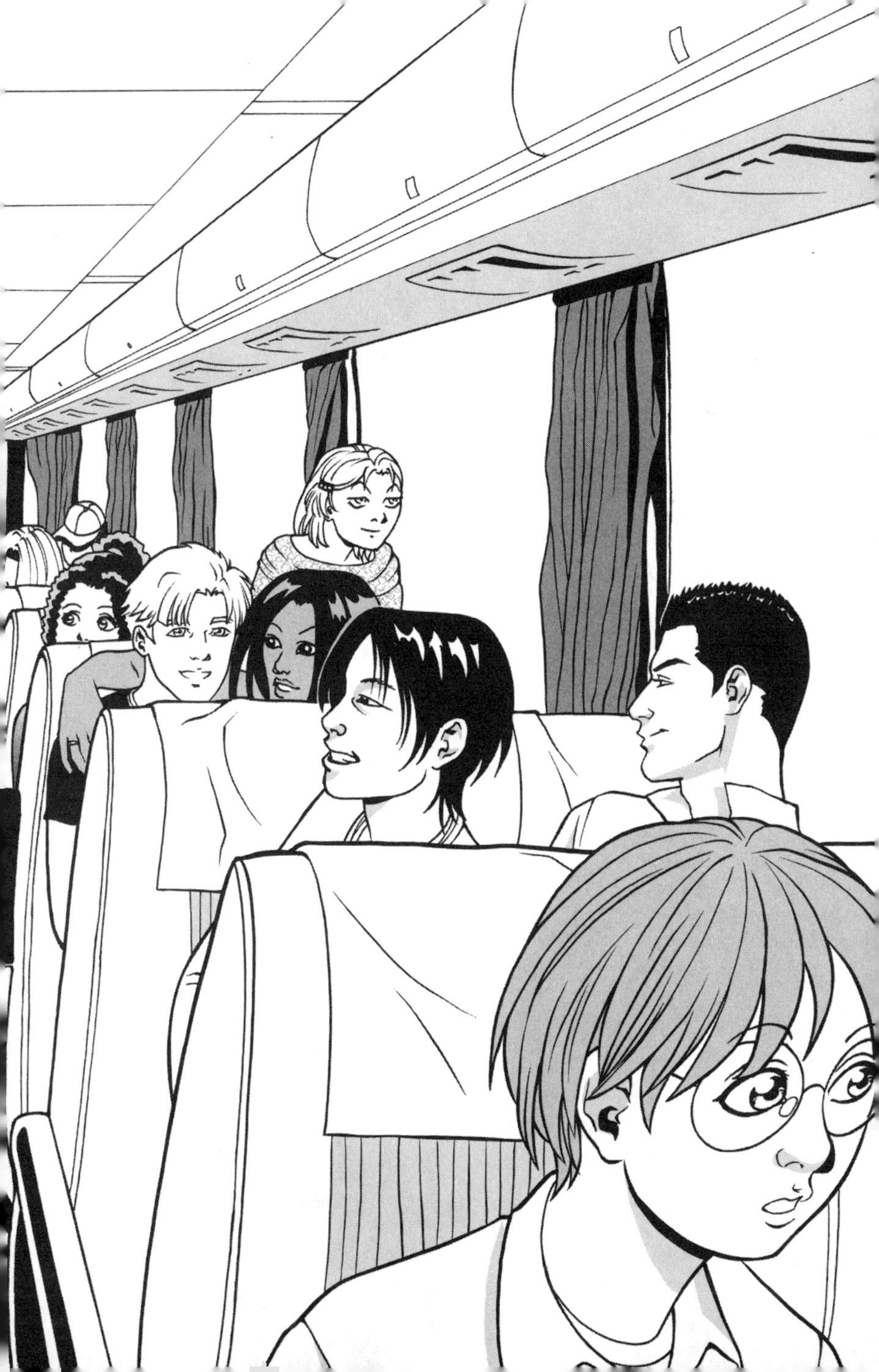

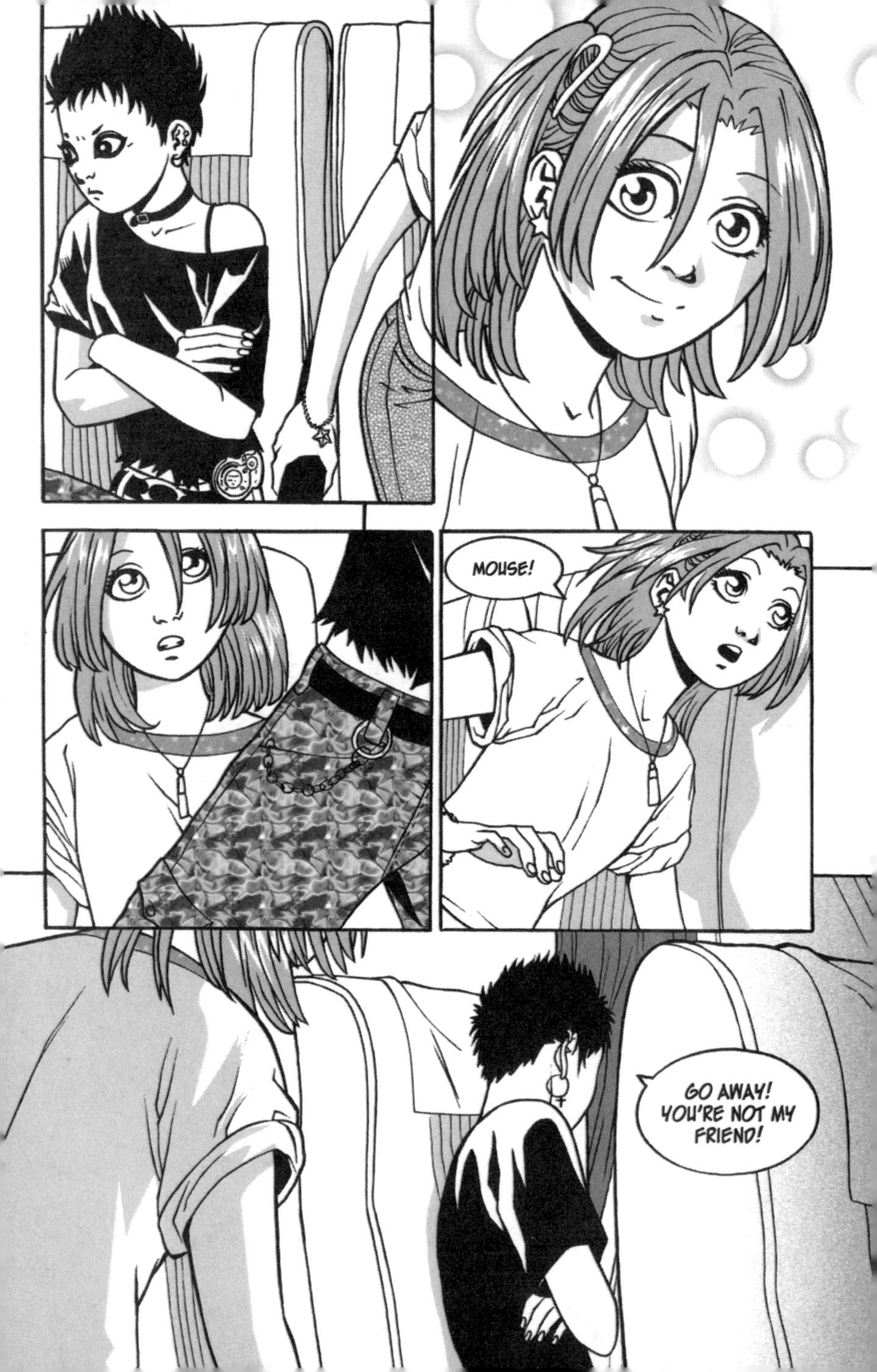
MOUSE!
GO AWAY! YOU'RE NOT MY FRIEND!

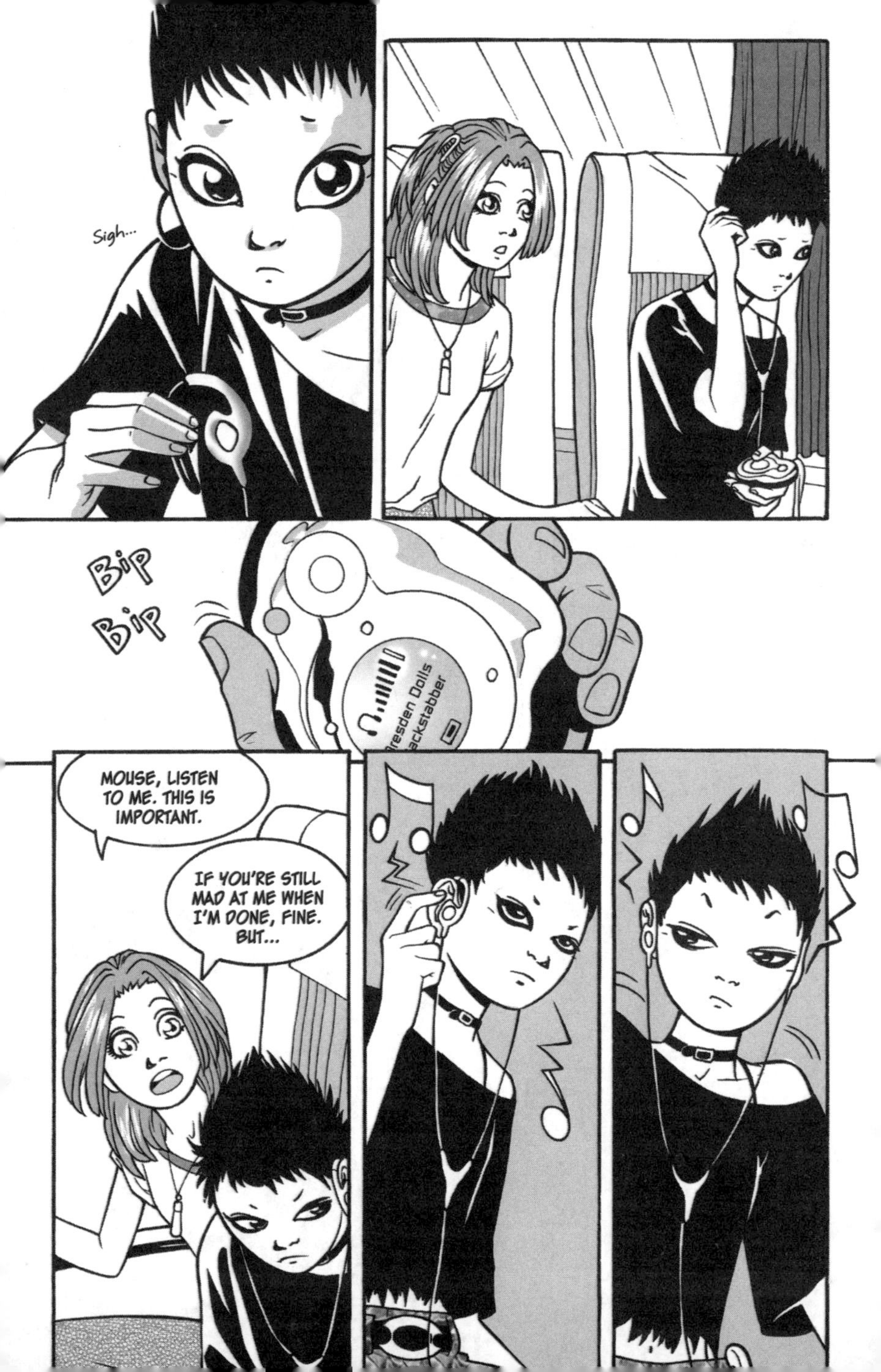
Sigh...
Bip
Bip
Dresden Dolls
Backstabber
MOUSE, LISTEN TO ME. THIS IS IMPORTANT.
IF YOU'RE STILL MAD AT ME WHEN I'M DONE, FINE. BUT...

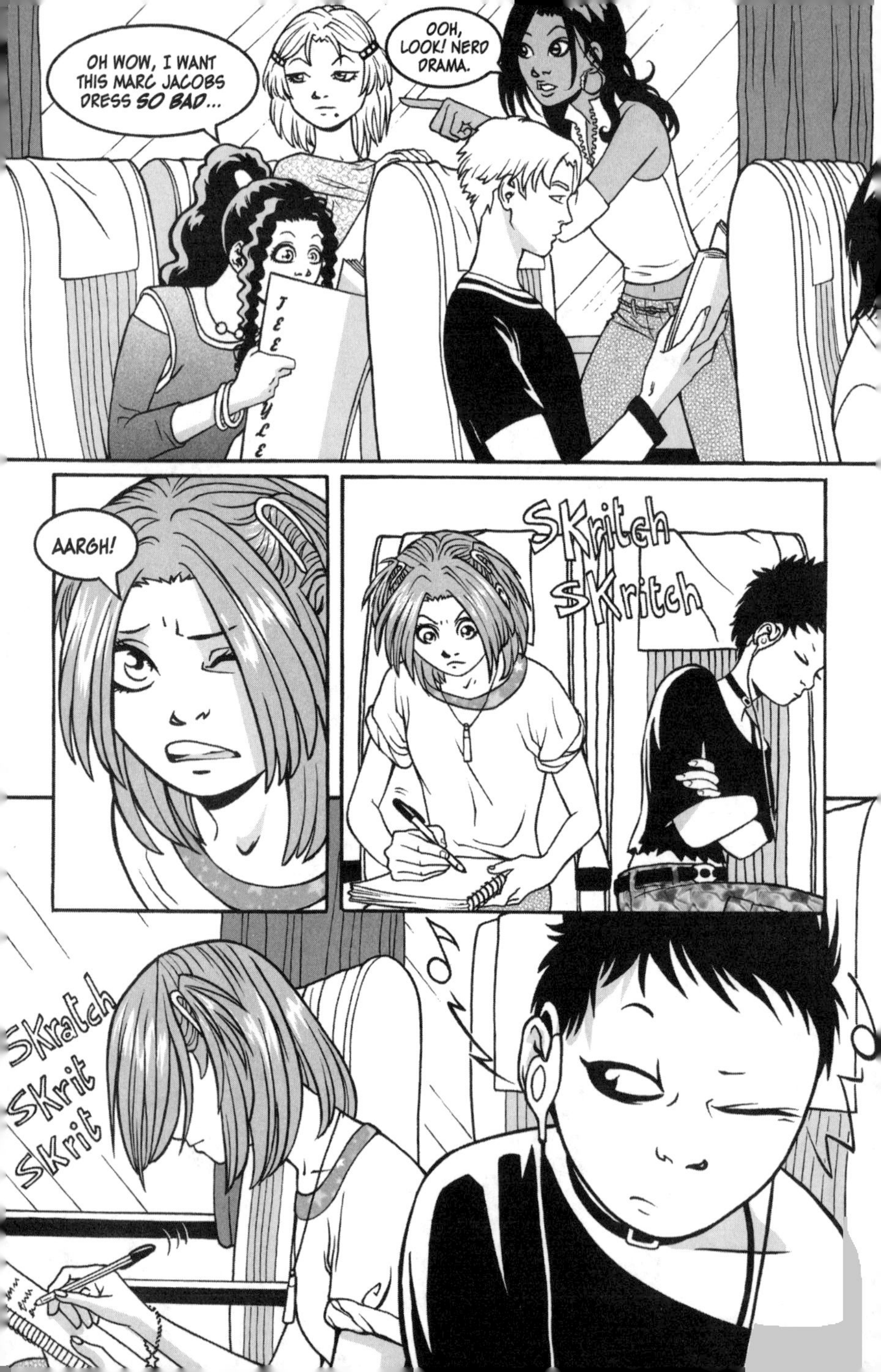
OH WOW, I WANT THIS MARC JACOBS DRESS SO BAD...
OOH, LOOK! NERD DRAMA.
AARGH!
SKritch
sKritch
SKratch
SKrit
SKrit

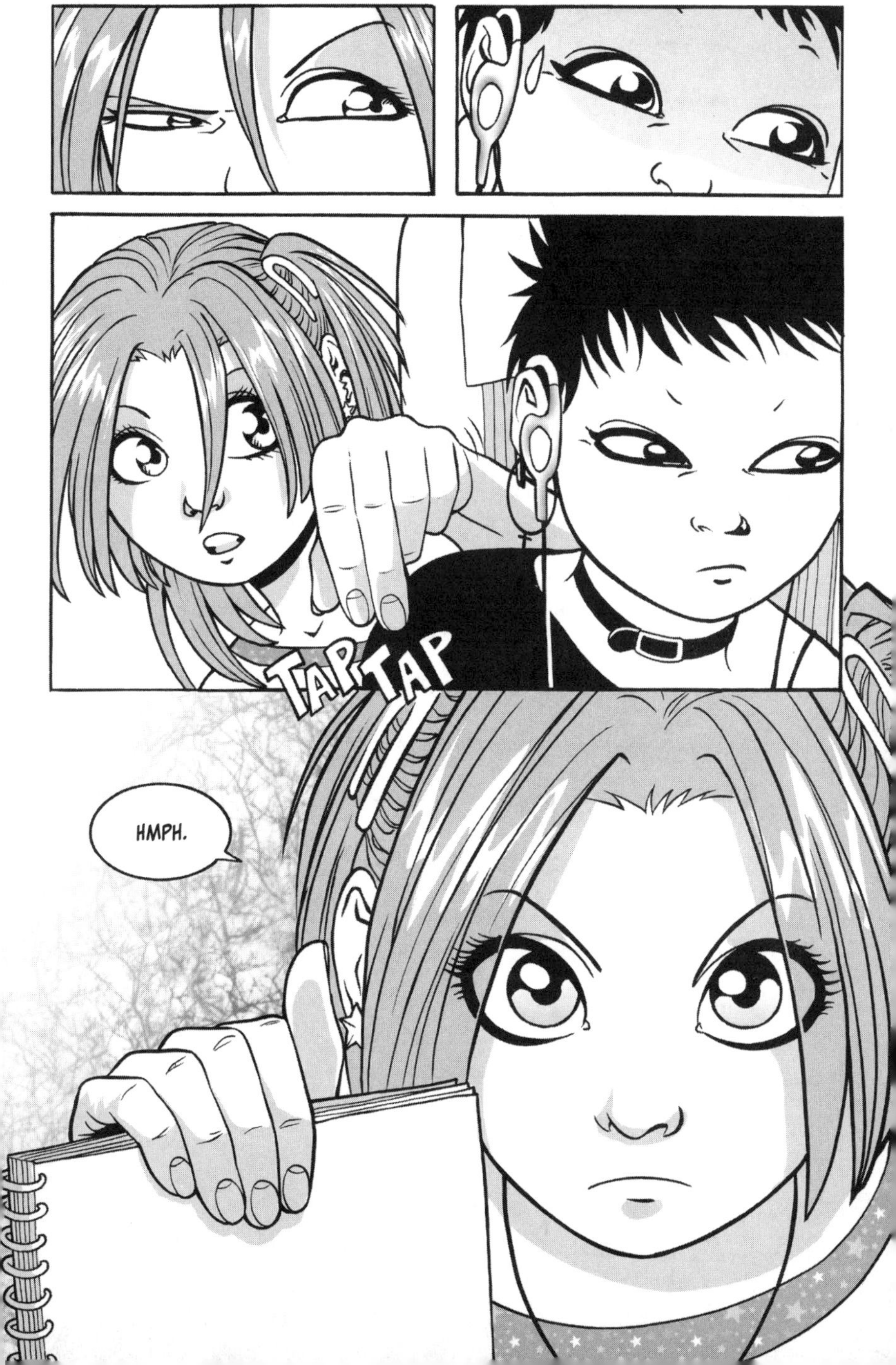
TAP TAP
HMPH.

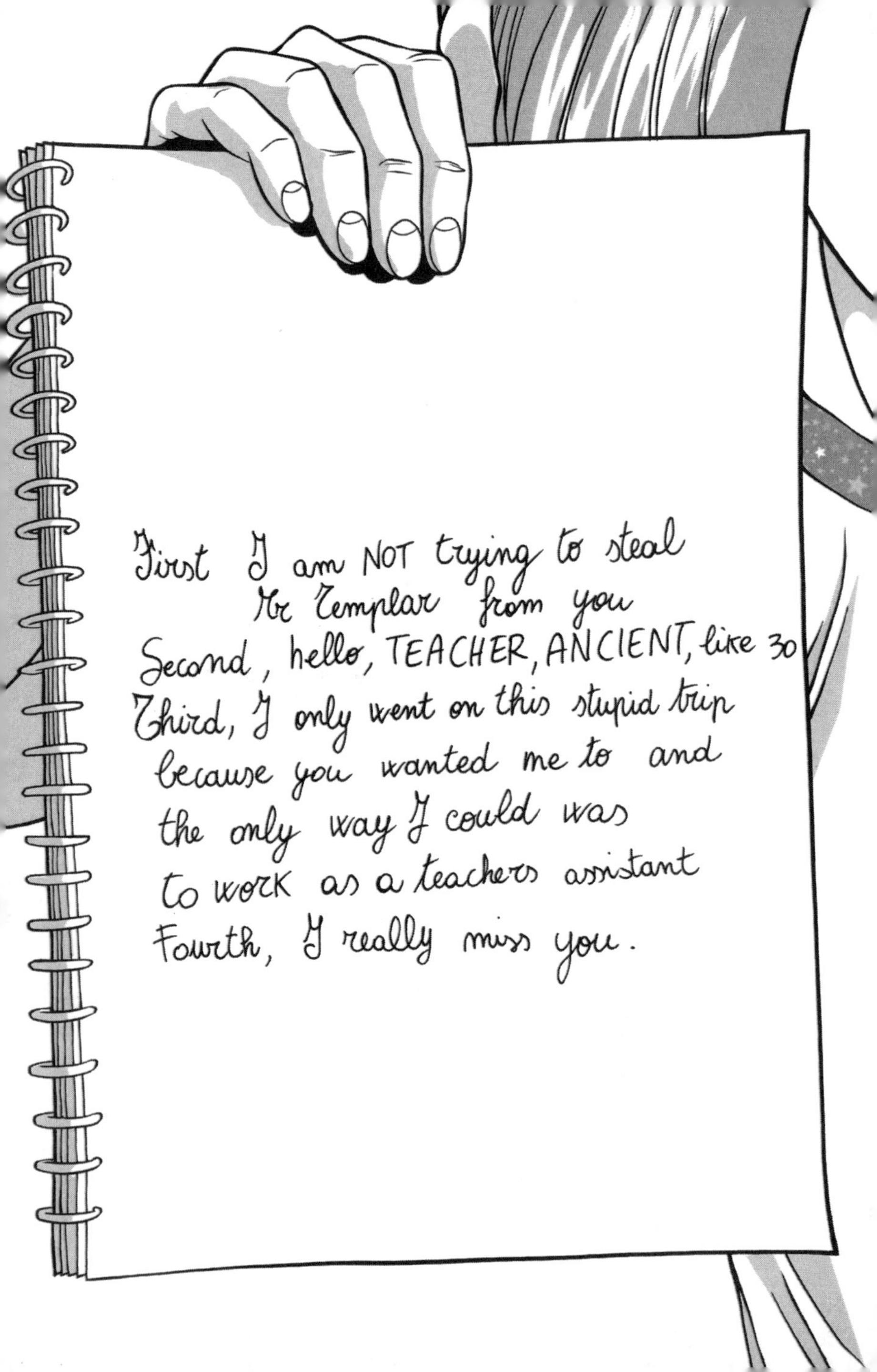
First I am NOT trying to steal
Mr Templar from you
Second, hello, TEACHER, ANCIENT, like 30
Third, I only went on this stupid trip
because you wanted me to and
the only way I could was
to work as a teachers assistant
Fourth, I really miss you.

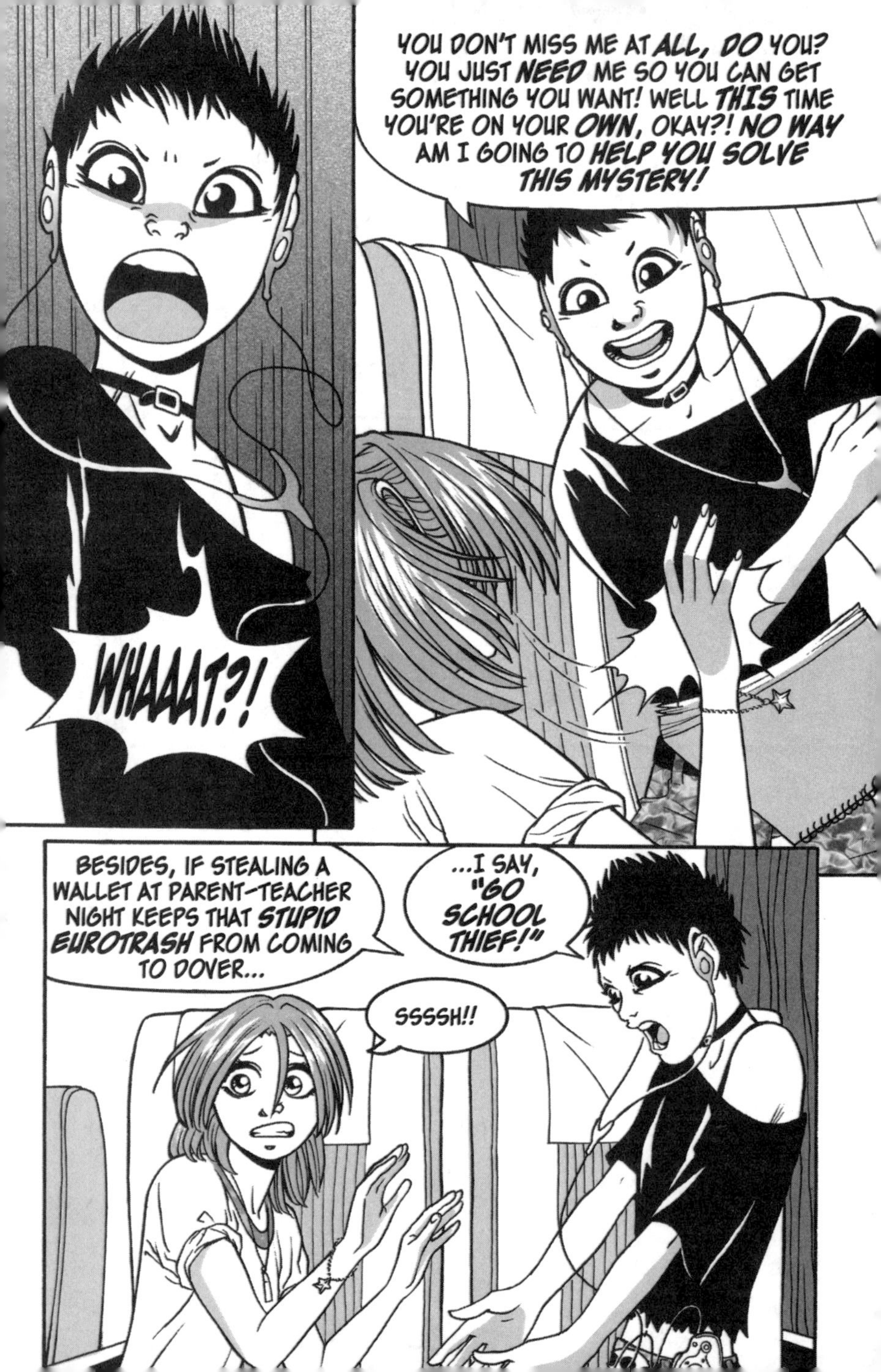
YOU DON'T MISS ME AT ALL, DO YOU? YOU JUST NEED ME SO YOU CAN GET SOMETHING YOU WANT! WELL THIS TIME YOU'RE ON YOUR OWN, OKAY?! NO WAY AM I GOING TO HELP YOU SOLVE THIS MYSTERY!
WHAAAT?!
BESIDES, IF STEALING A WALLET AT PARENT-TEACHER NIGHT KEEPS THAT STUPID EUROTRASH FROM COMING TO DOVER...
...I SAY, "GO SCHOOL THIEF!"
SSSSH!!

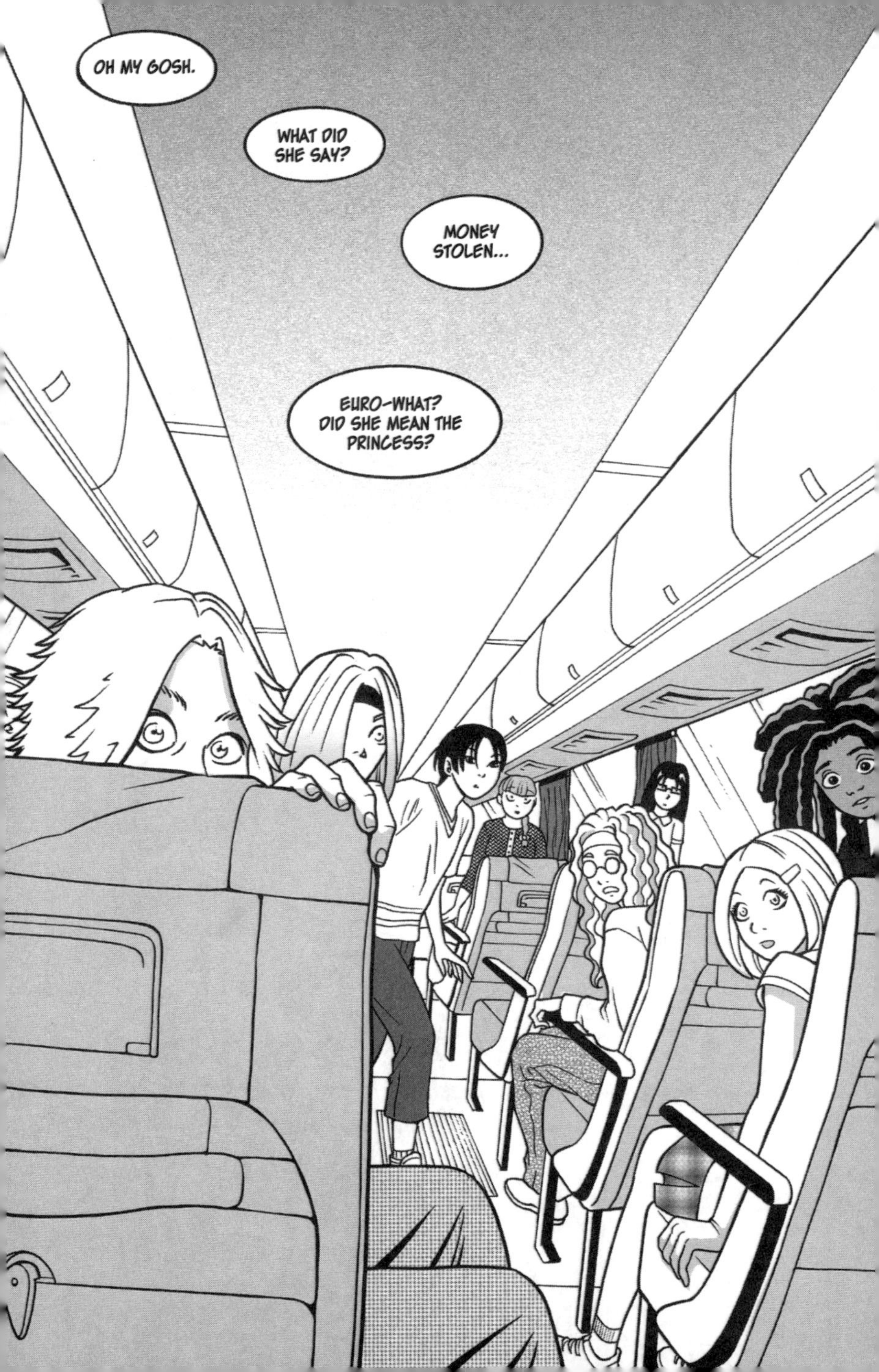
OH MY GOSH.
WHAT DID SHE SAY?
MONEY STOLEN...
EURO-WHAT? DID SHE MEAN THE PRINCESS?

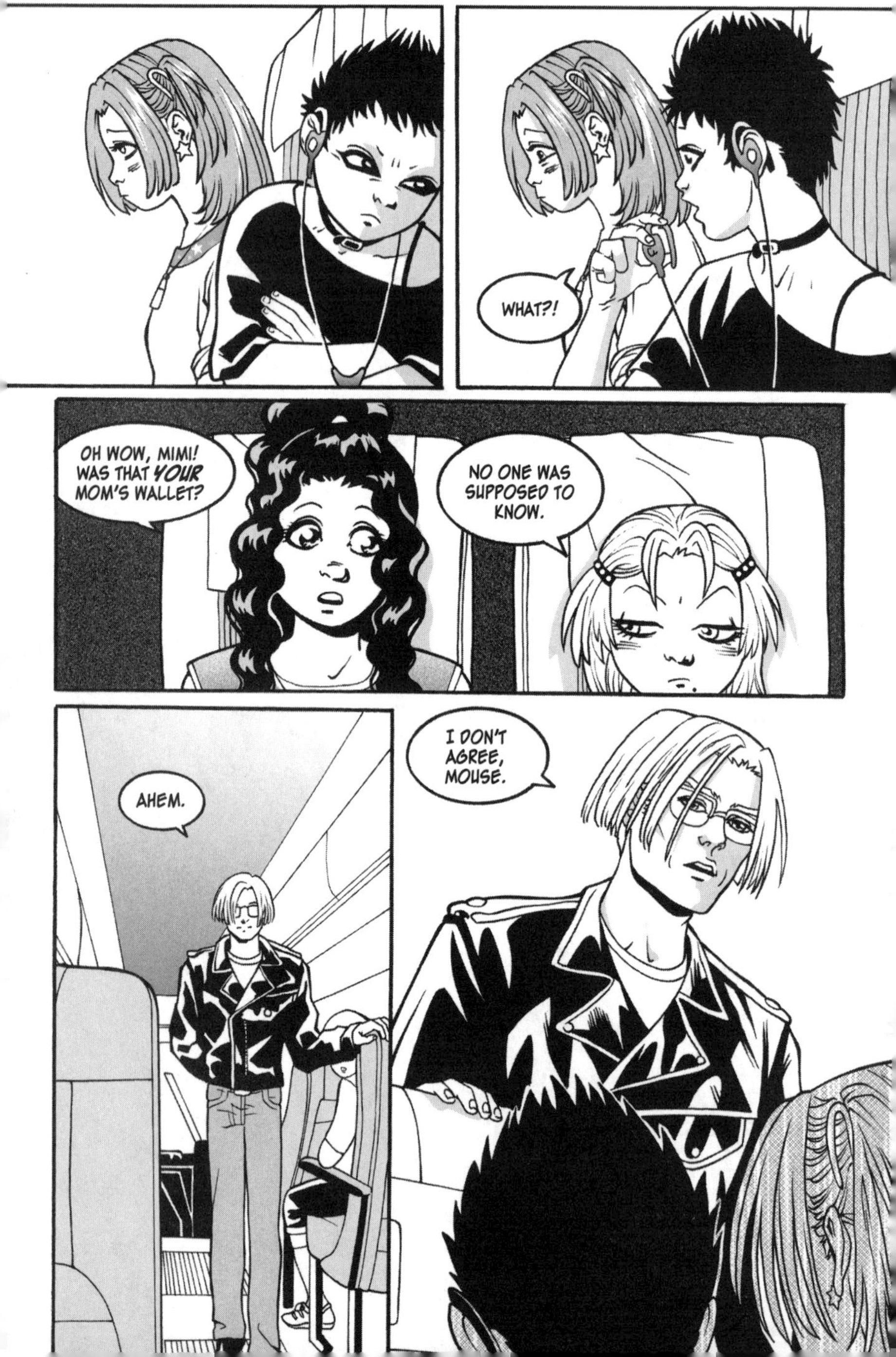
WHAT?!
OH WOW, MIMI! WAS THAT YOUR MOM'S WALLET?
NO ONE WAS SUPPOSED TO KNOW.
AHEM.
I DON'T AGREE, MOUSE.

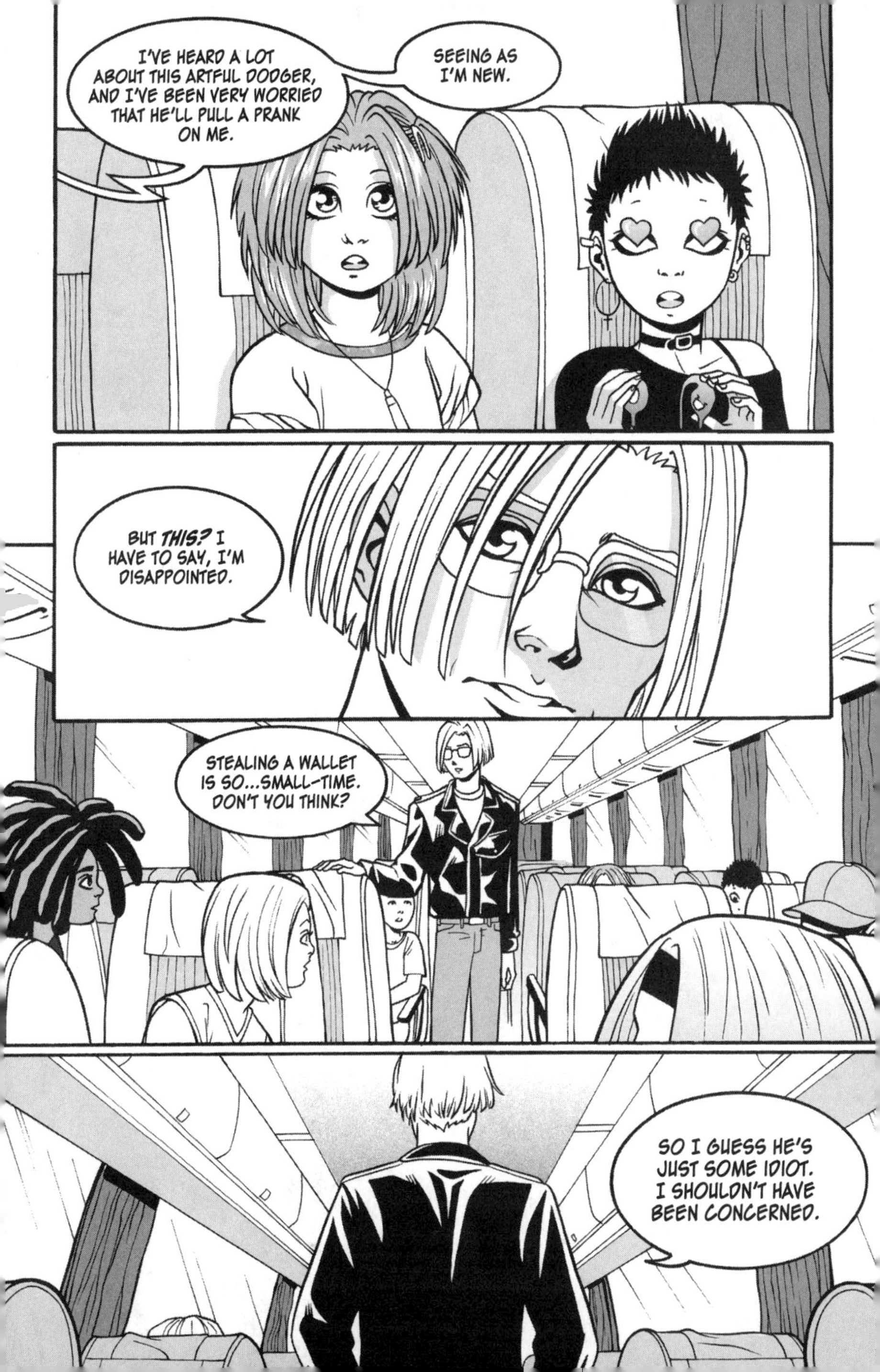
I'VE HEARD A LOT ABOUT THIS ARTFUL DODGER, AND I'VE BEEN VERY WORRIED THAT HE'LL PULL A PRANK ON ME.
SEEING AS I'M NEW.
BUT *THIS?* I HAVE TO SAY, I'M DISAPPOINTED.
STEALING A WALLET IS SO...SMALL-TIME. DON'T YOU THINK?
SO I GUESS HE'S JUST SOME IDIOT. I SHOULDN'T HAVE BEEN CONCERNED.

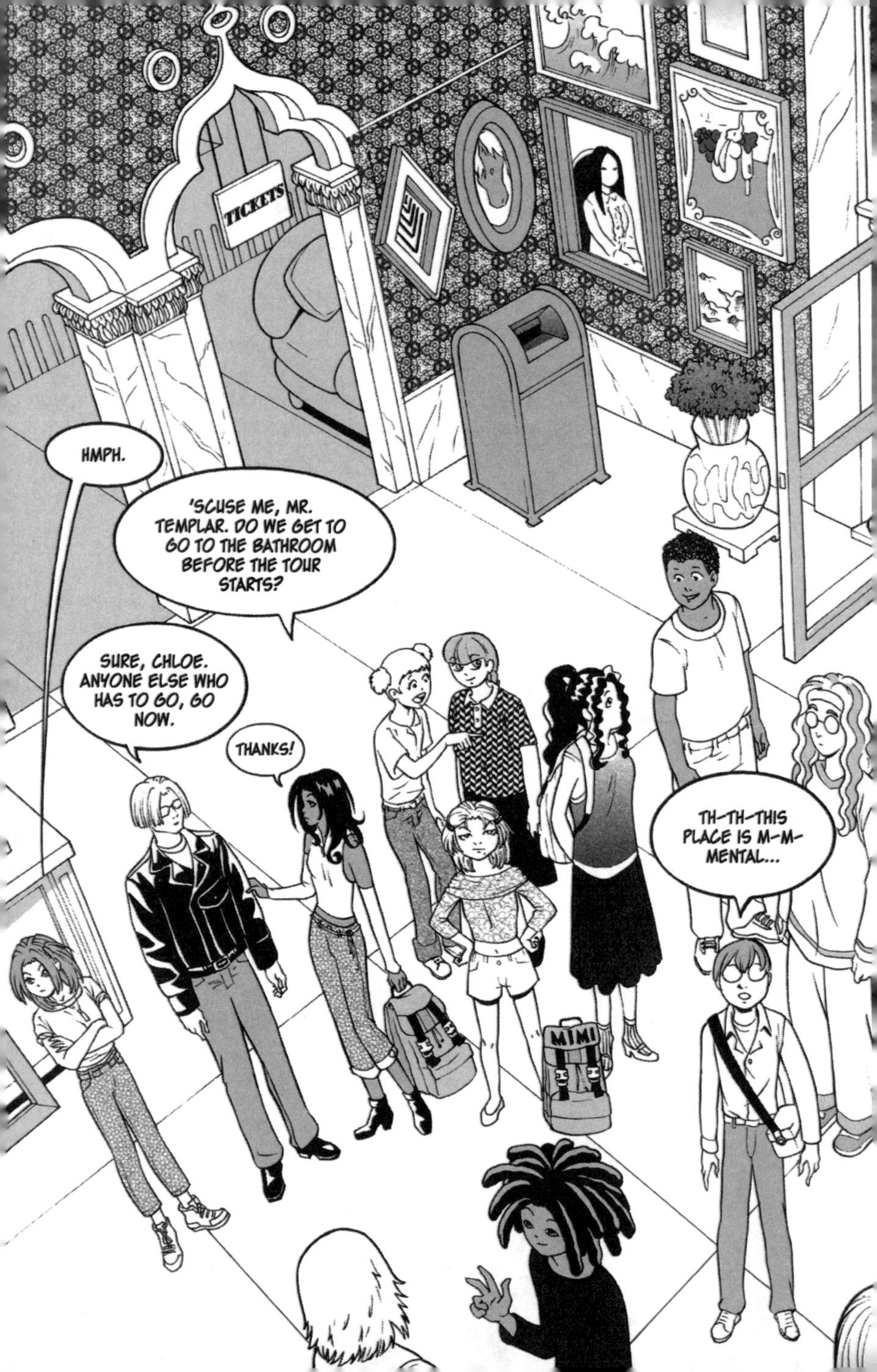
TICKETS
HMPH.
'SCUSE ME, MR. TEMPLAR. DO WE GET TO GO TO THE BATHROOM BEFORE THE TOUR STARTS?
SURE, CHLOE. ANYONE ELSE WHO HAS TO GO, GO NOW.
THANKS!
TH-TH-THIS PLACE IS M-M-MENTAL...
MIMI

Chapter 3: Framed

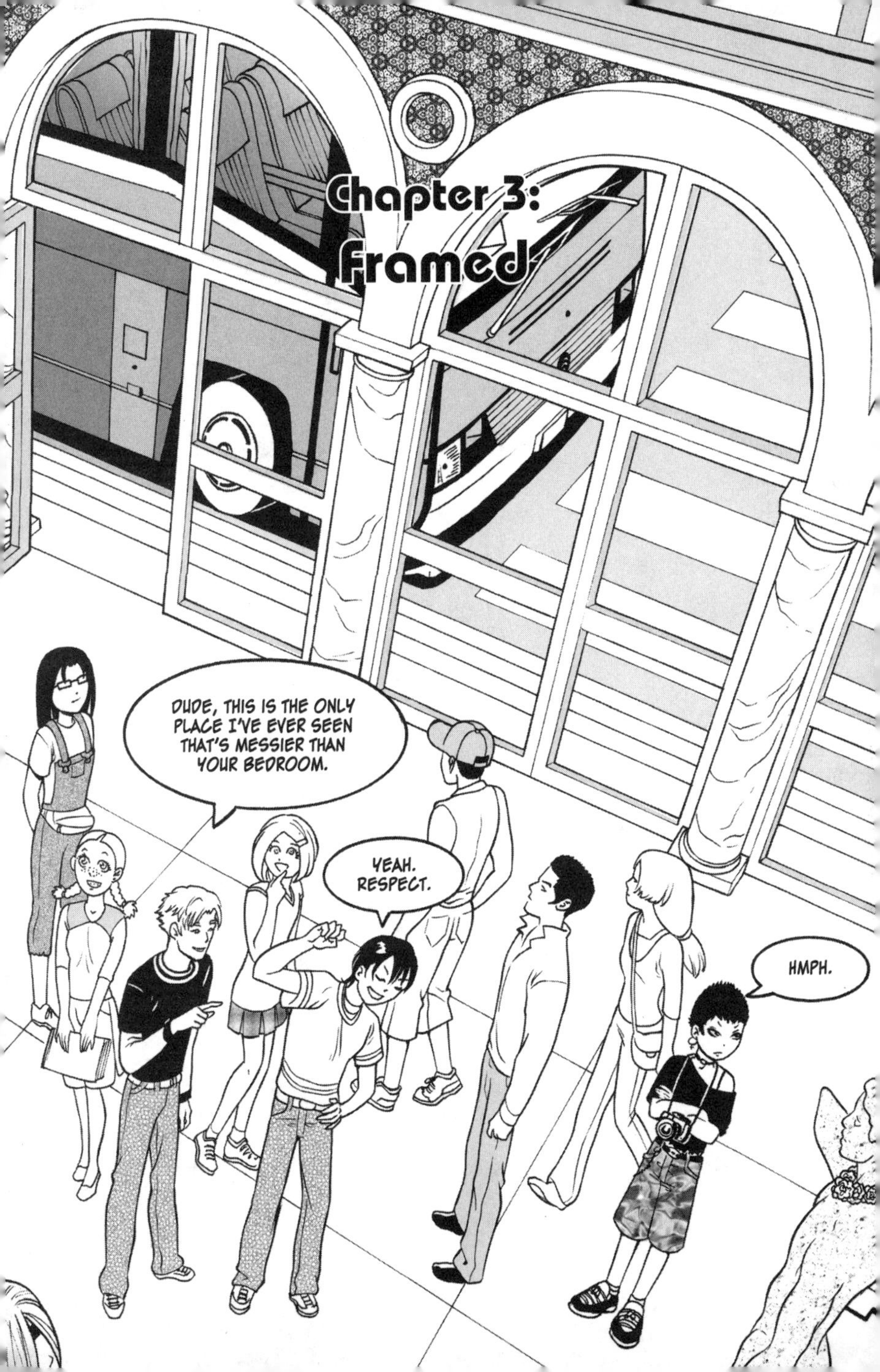
DUDE, THIS IS THE ONLY PLACE I'VE EVER SEEN THAT'S MESSIER THAN YOUR BEDROOM.
YEAH. RESPECT.
HMPH.

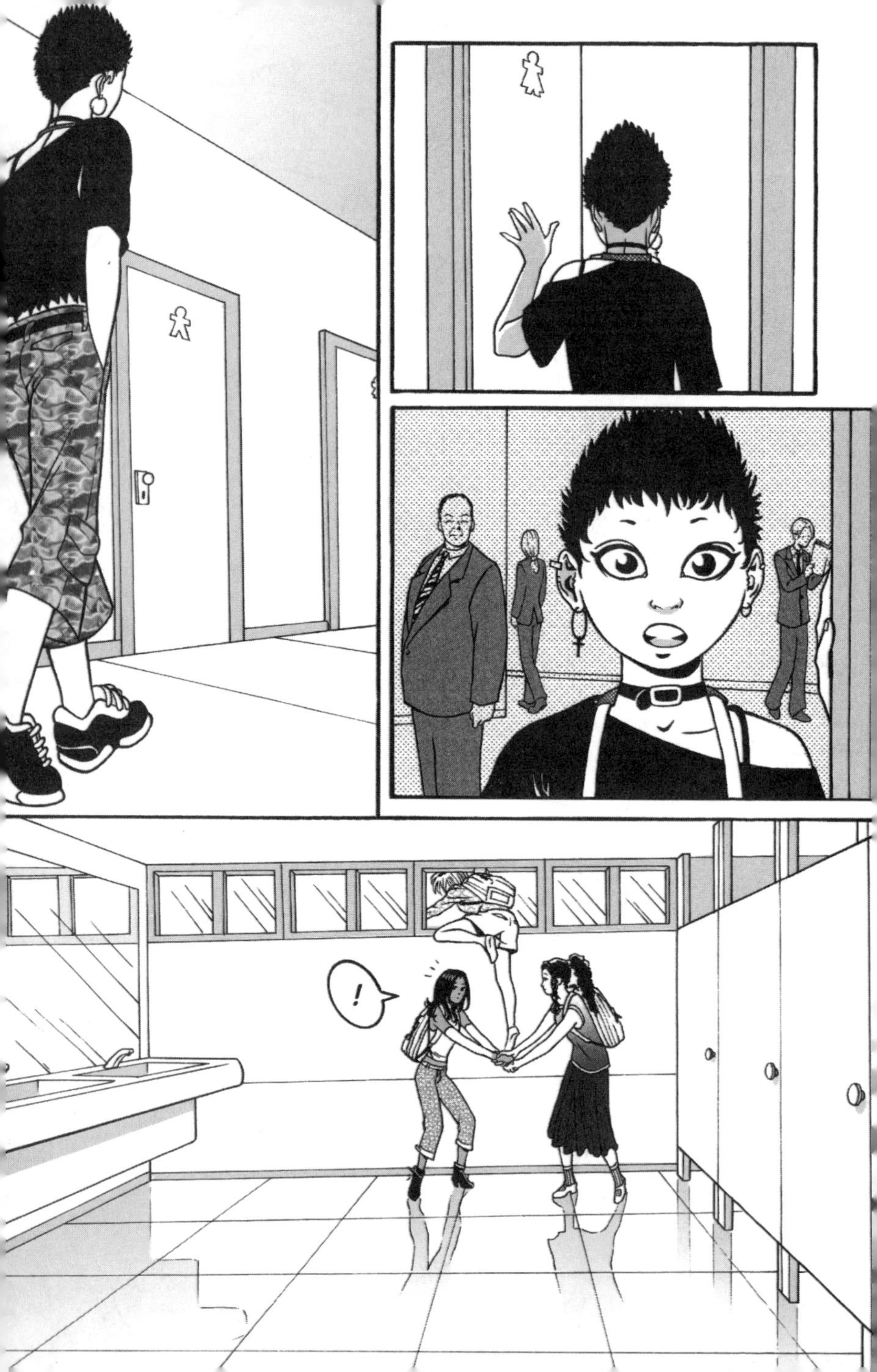
!

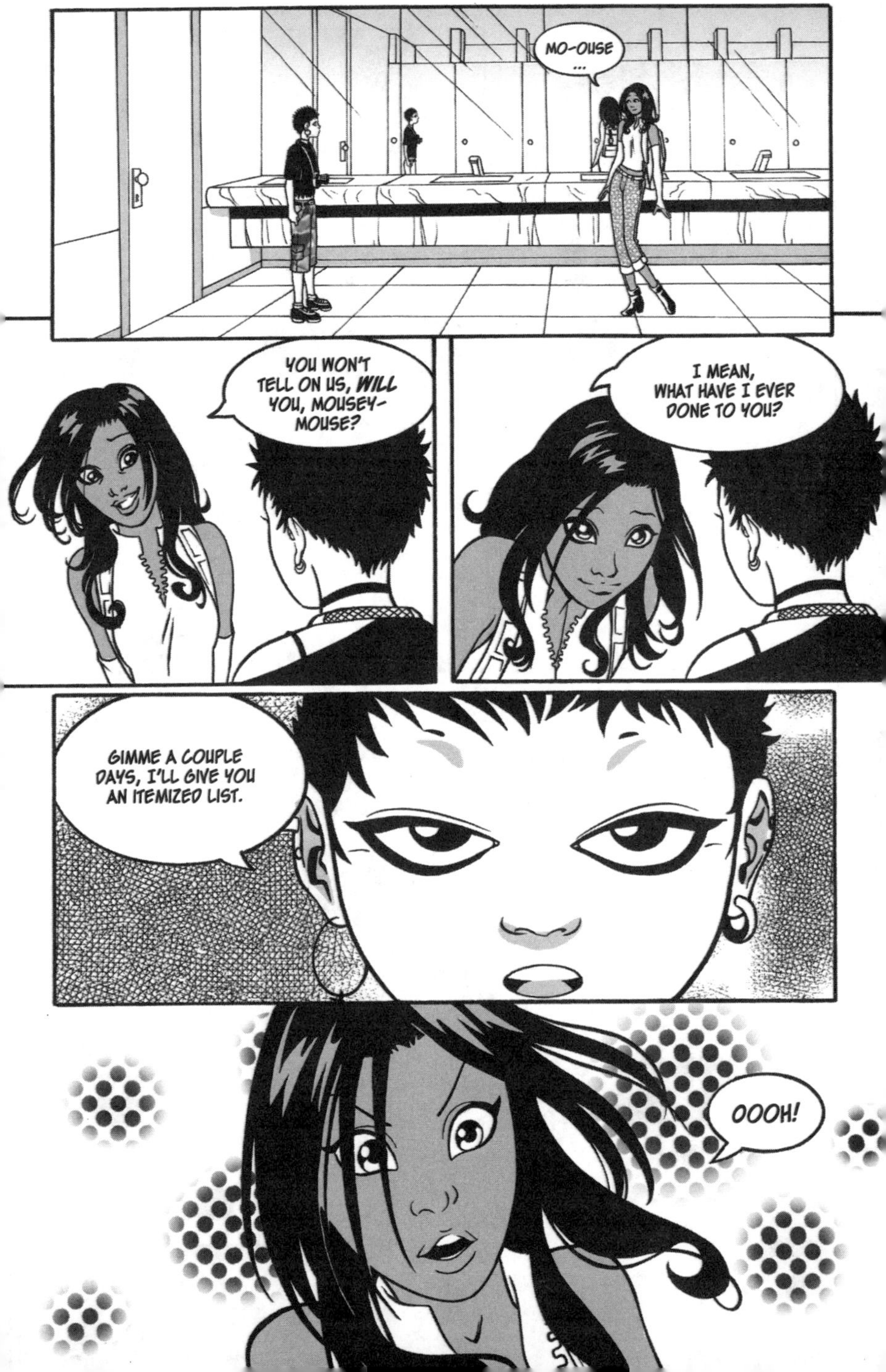
MO-OUSE ...
YOU WON'T TELL ON US, WILL YOU, MOUSEY-MOUSE?
I MEAN, WHAT HAVE I EVER DONE TO YOU?
GIMME A COUPLE DAYS, I'LL GIVE YOU AN ITEMIZED LIST.
OOOH!

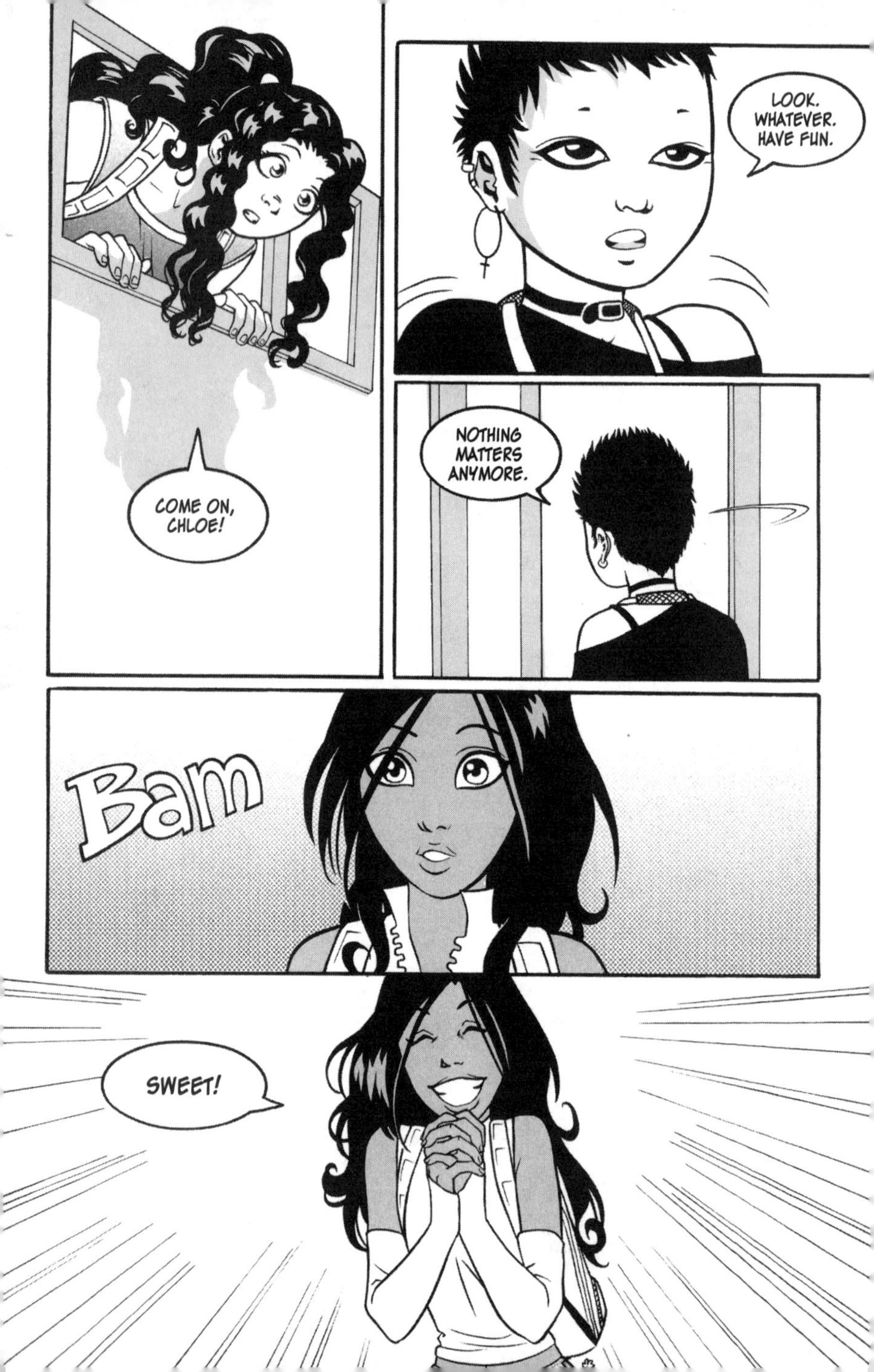
COME ON, CHLOE!
LOOK. WHATEVER. HAVE FUN.
NOTHING MATTERS ANYMORE.
Bam
SWEET!

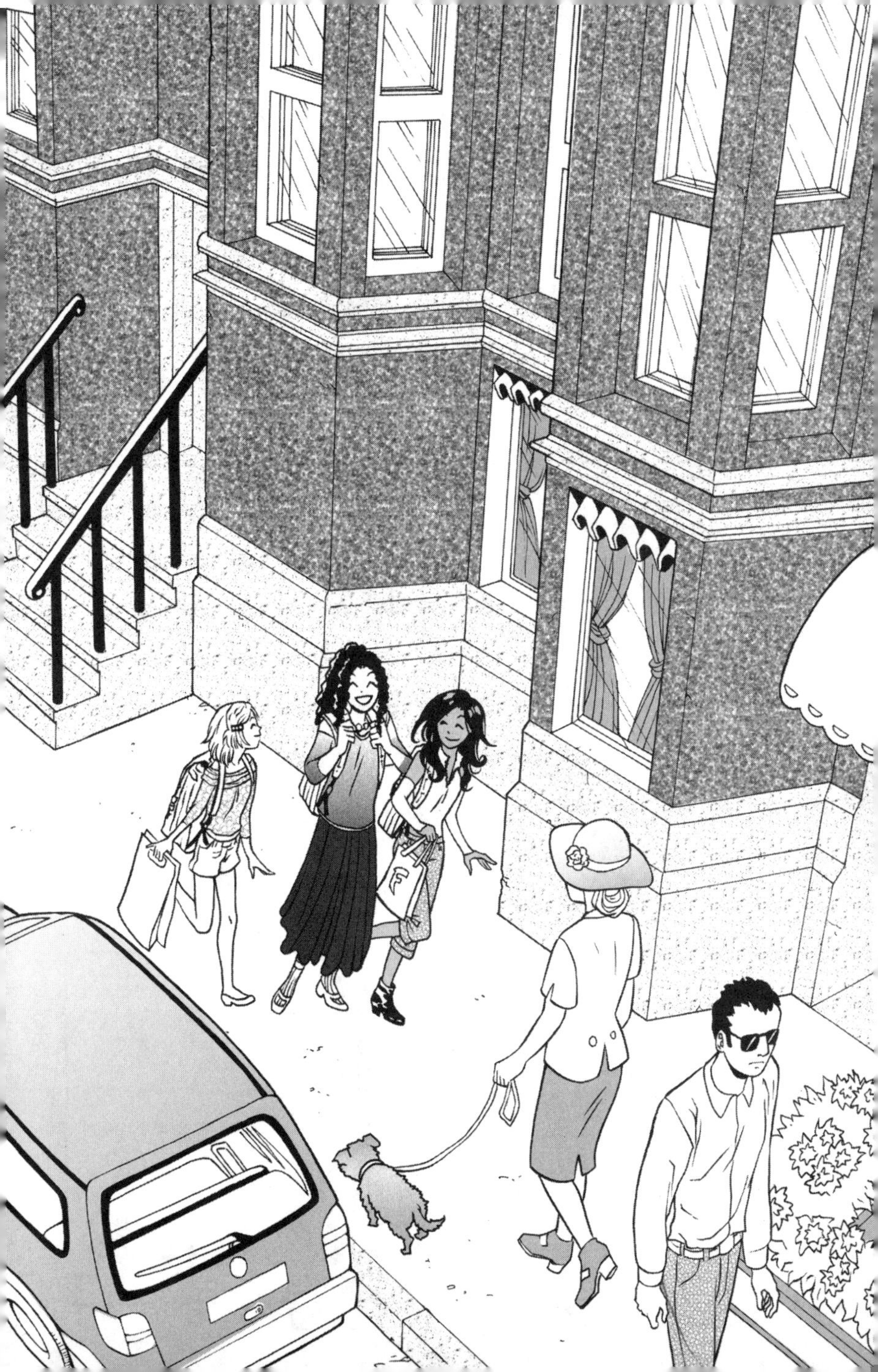

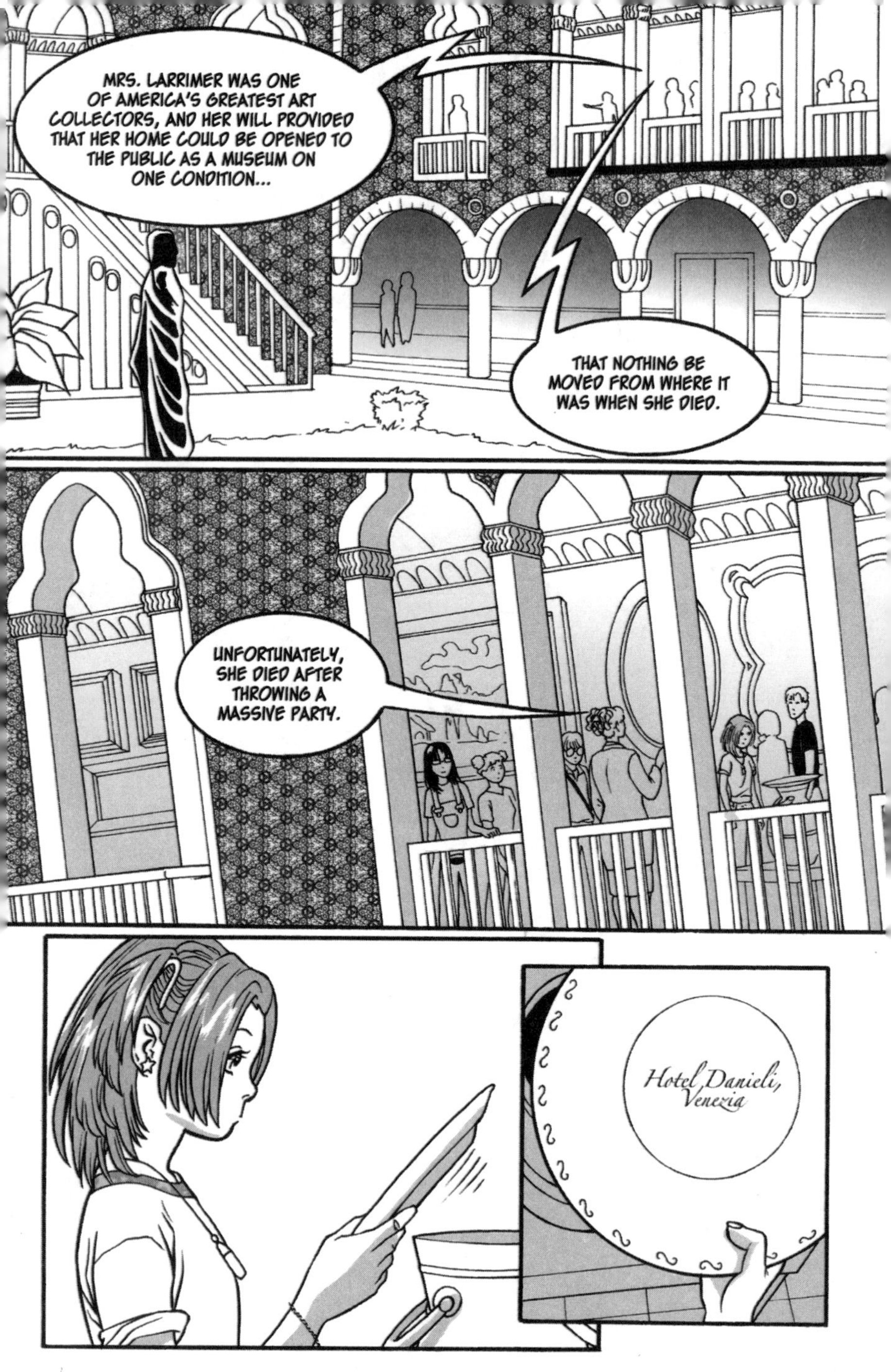
MRS. LARRIMER WAS ONE OF AMERICA'S GREATEST ART COLLECTORS, AND HER WILL PROVIDED THAT HER HOME COULD BE OPENED TO THE PUBLIC AS A MUSEUM ON ONE CONDITION...
THAT NOTHING BE MOVED FROM WHERE IT WAS WHEN SHE DIED.
UNFORTUNATELY, SHE DIED AFTER THROWING A MASSIVE PARTY.
Hotel Danieli, Venezia

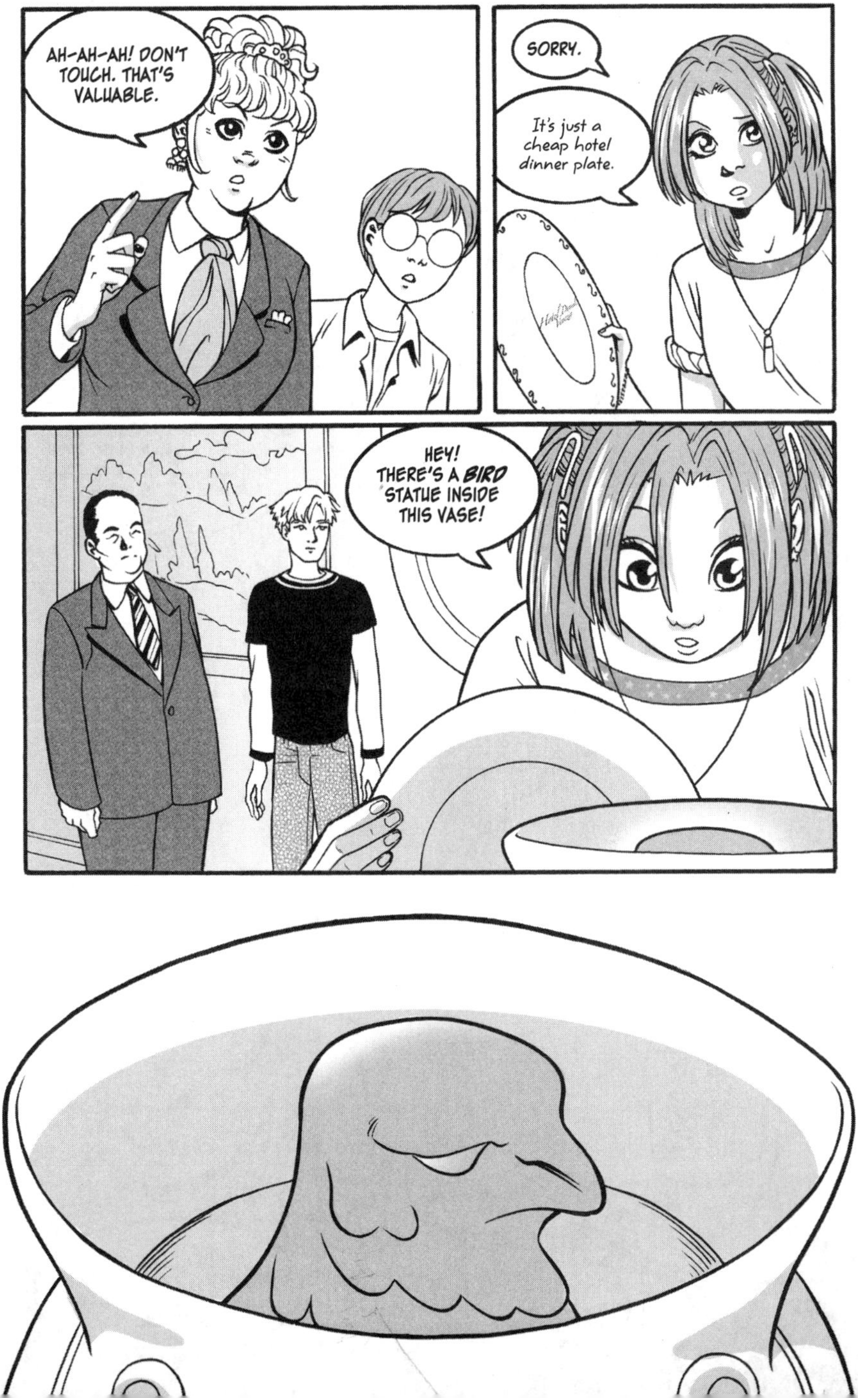
AH-AH-AH! DON'T TOUCH. THAT'S VALUABLE.
SORRY.
It's just a cheap hotel dinner plate.
HEY! THERE'S A BIRD STATUE INSIDE THIS VASE!

51

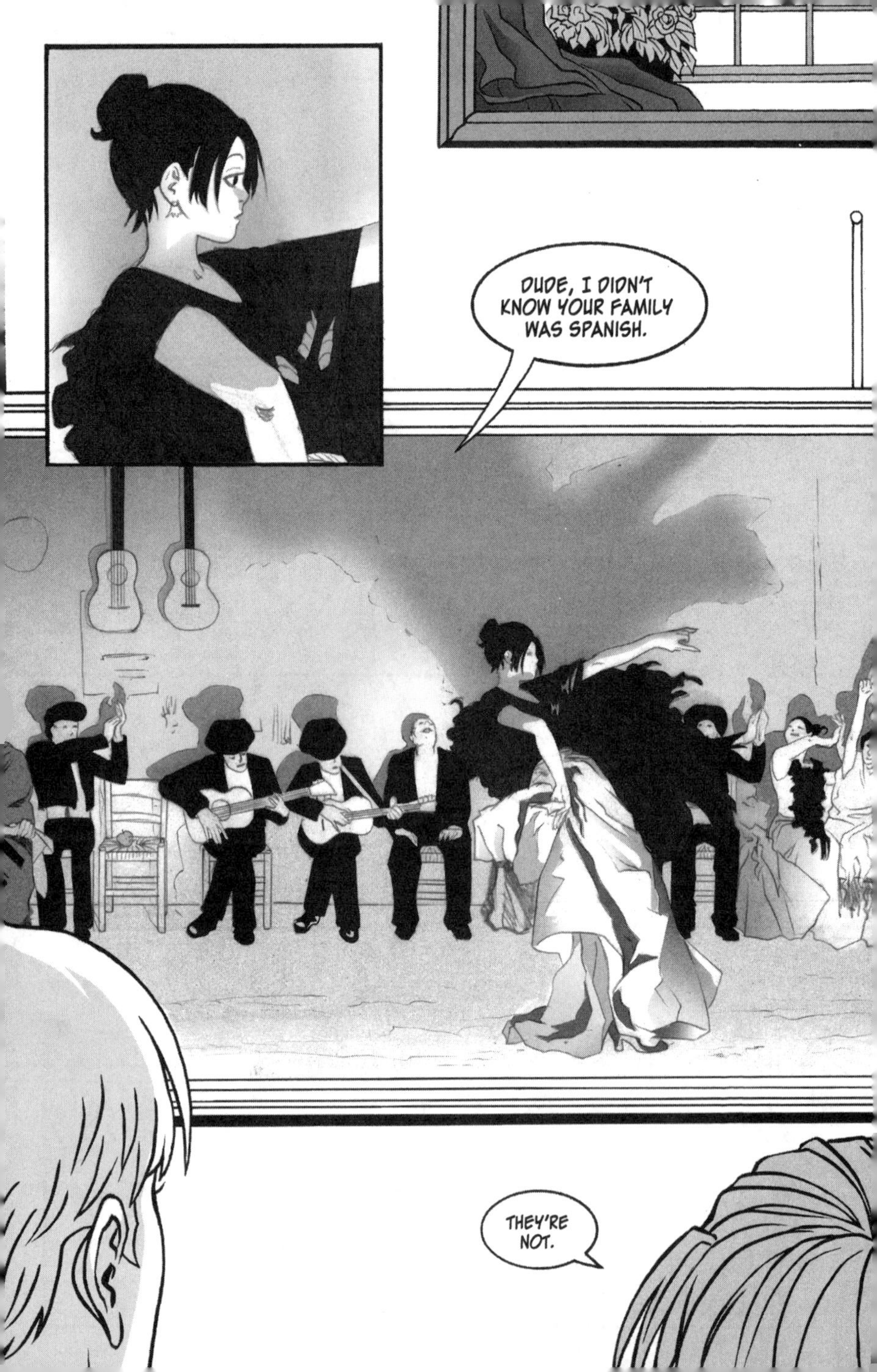
DUDE, I DIDN'T KNOW YOUR FAMILY WAS SPANISH.
THEY'RE NOT.

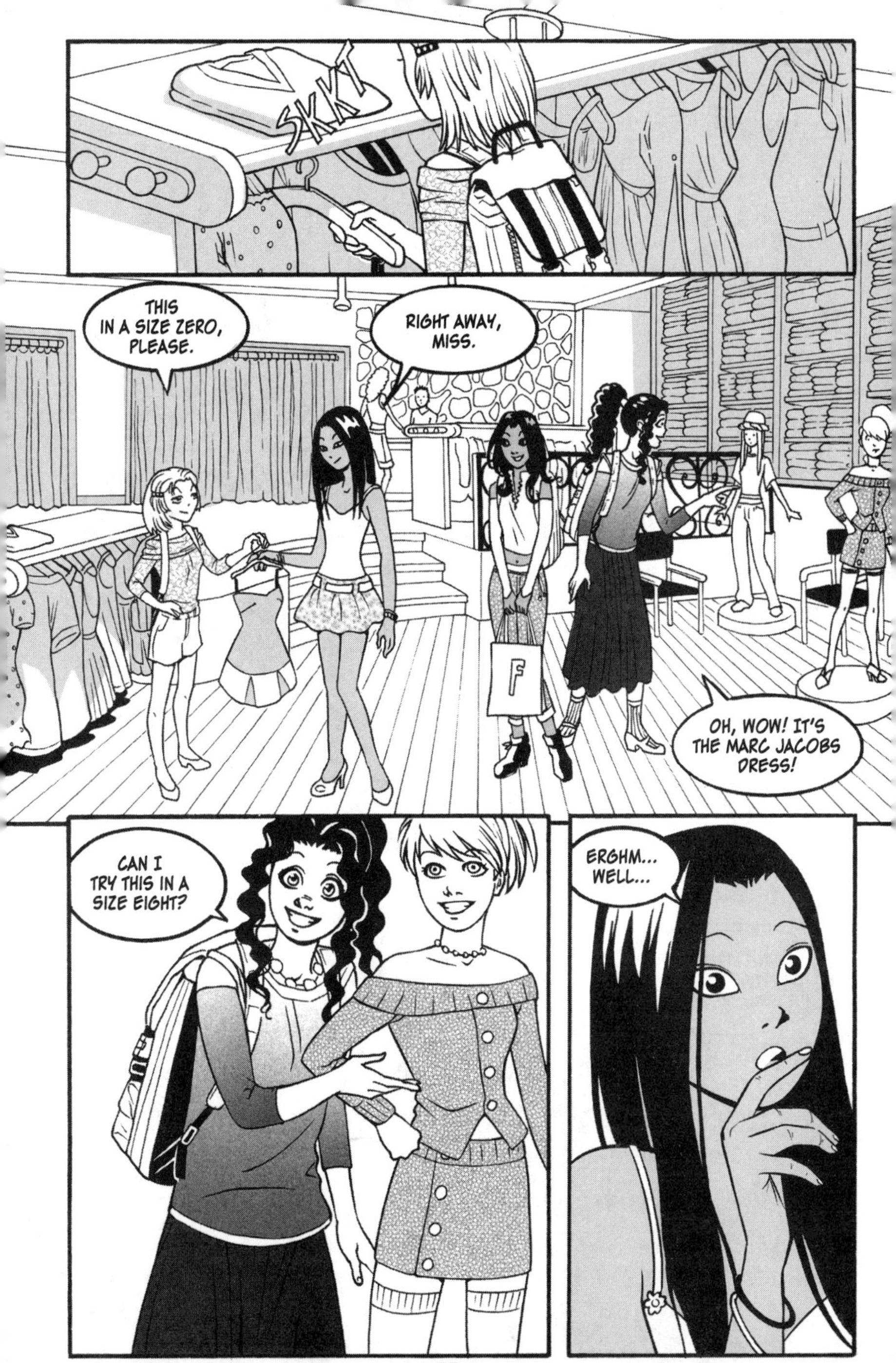
SKKT
THIS IN A SIZE ZERO, PLEASE.
RIGHT AWAY, MISS.
OH, WOW! IT'S THE MARC JACOBS DRESS!
CAN I TRY THIS IN A SIZE EIGHT?
ERGHM... WELL...

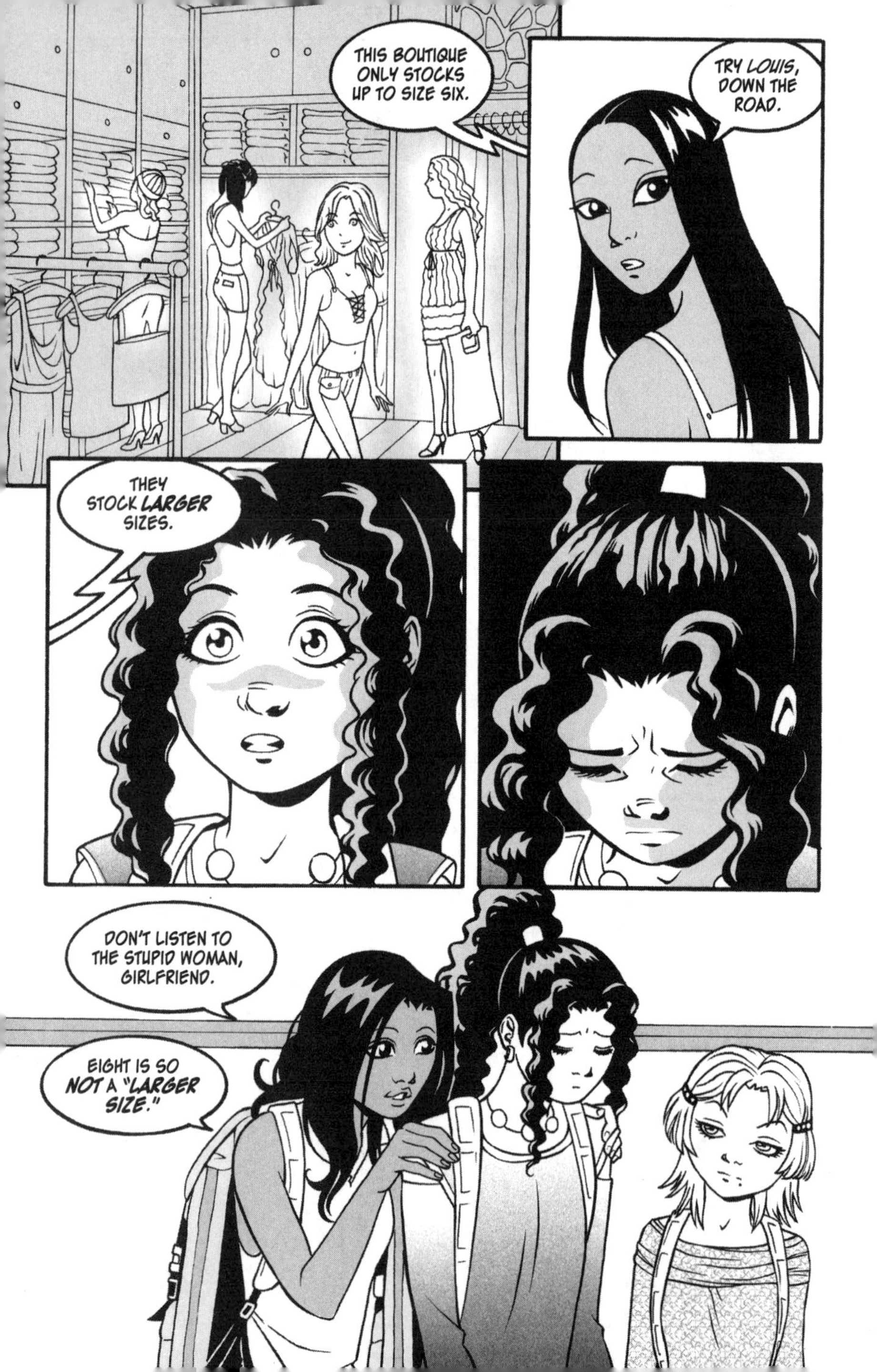
THIS BOUTIQUE ONLY STOCKS UP TO SIZE SIX.
TRY *LOUIS*, DOWN THE ROAD.
THEY STOCK **LARGER** SIZES.
DON'T LISTEN TO THE STUPID WOMAN, GIRLFRIEND.
EIGHT IS SO ***NOT*** A "***LARGER SIZE.***"

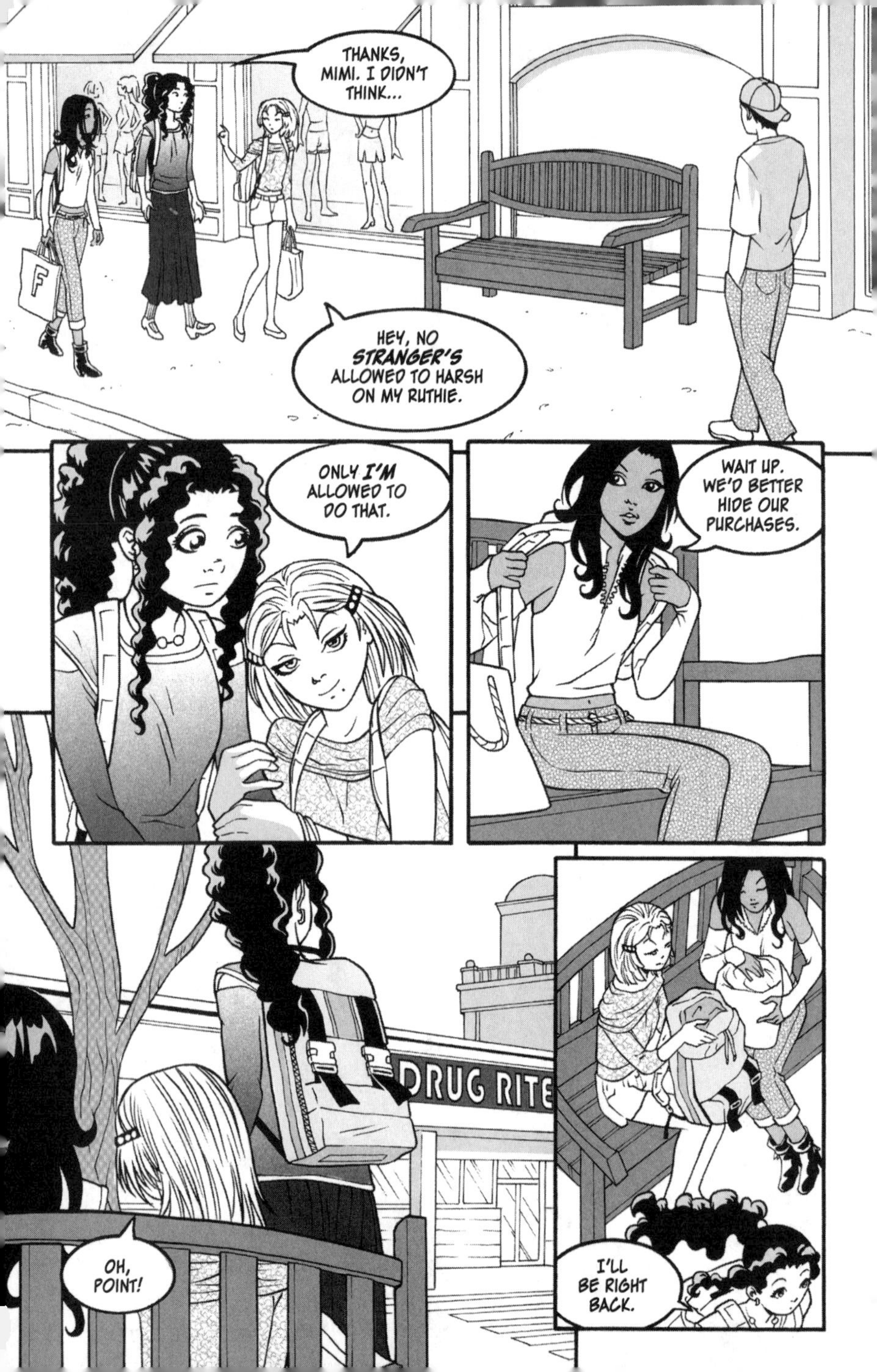
THANKS, MIMI. I DIDN'T THINK...
HEY, NO STRANGER'S ALLOWED TO HARSH ON MY RUTHIE.
ONLY I'M ALLOWED TO DO THAT.
WAIT UP. WE'D BETTER HIDE OUR PURCHASES.
DRUG RITE
OH, POINT!
I'LL BE RIGHT BACK.

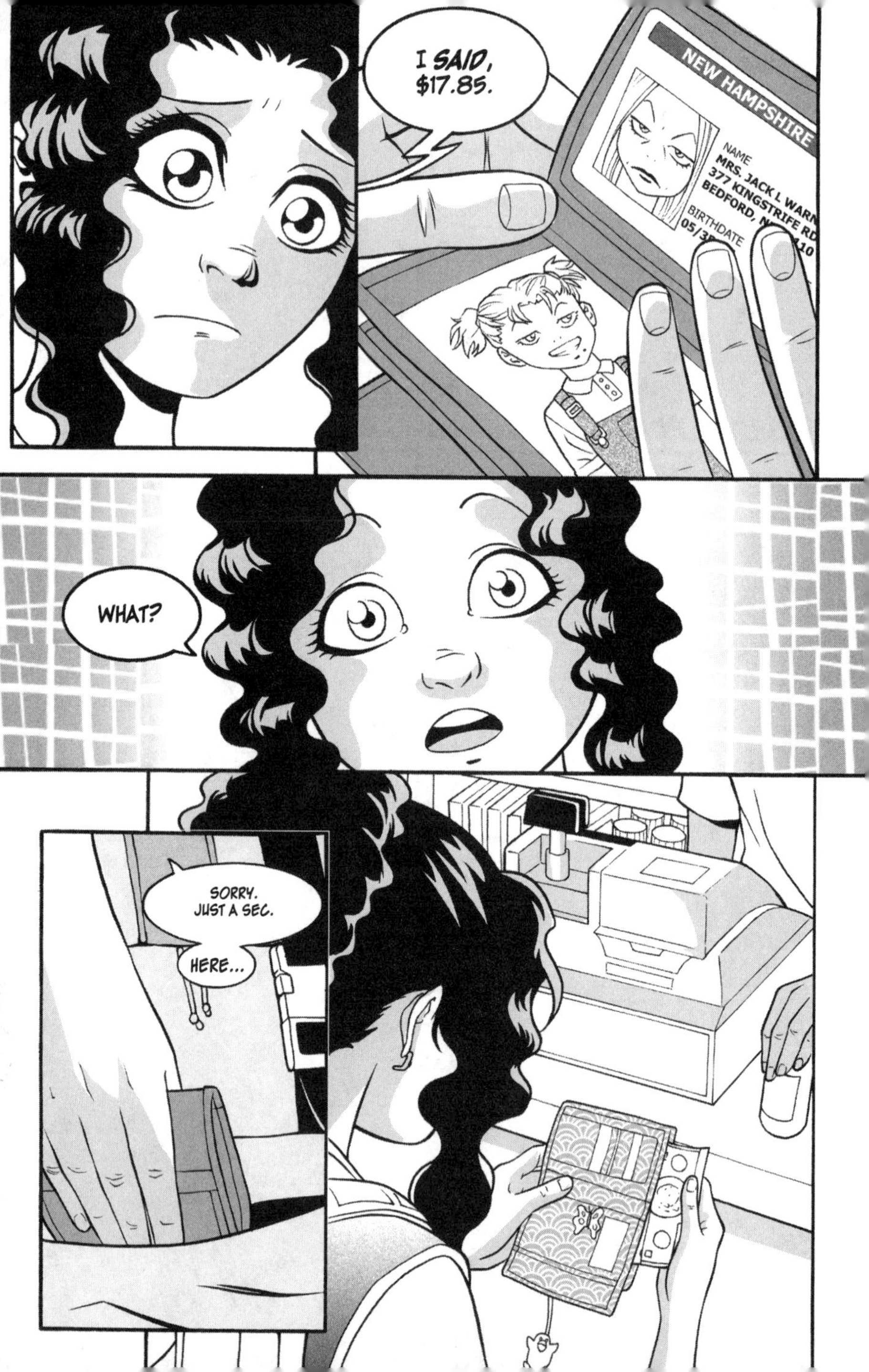
I SAID, $17.85.
NEW HAMPSHIRE
NAME
BIRTHDATE
WHAT?
SORRY. JUST A SEC.
HERE...

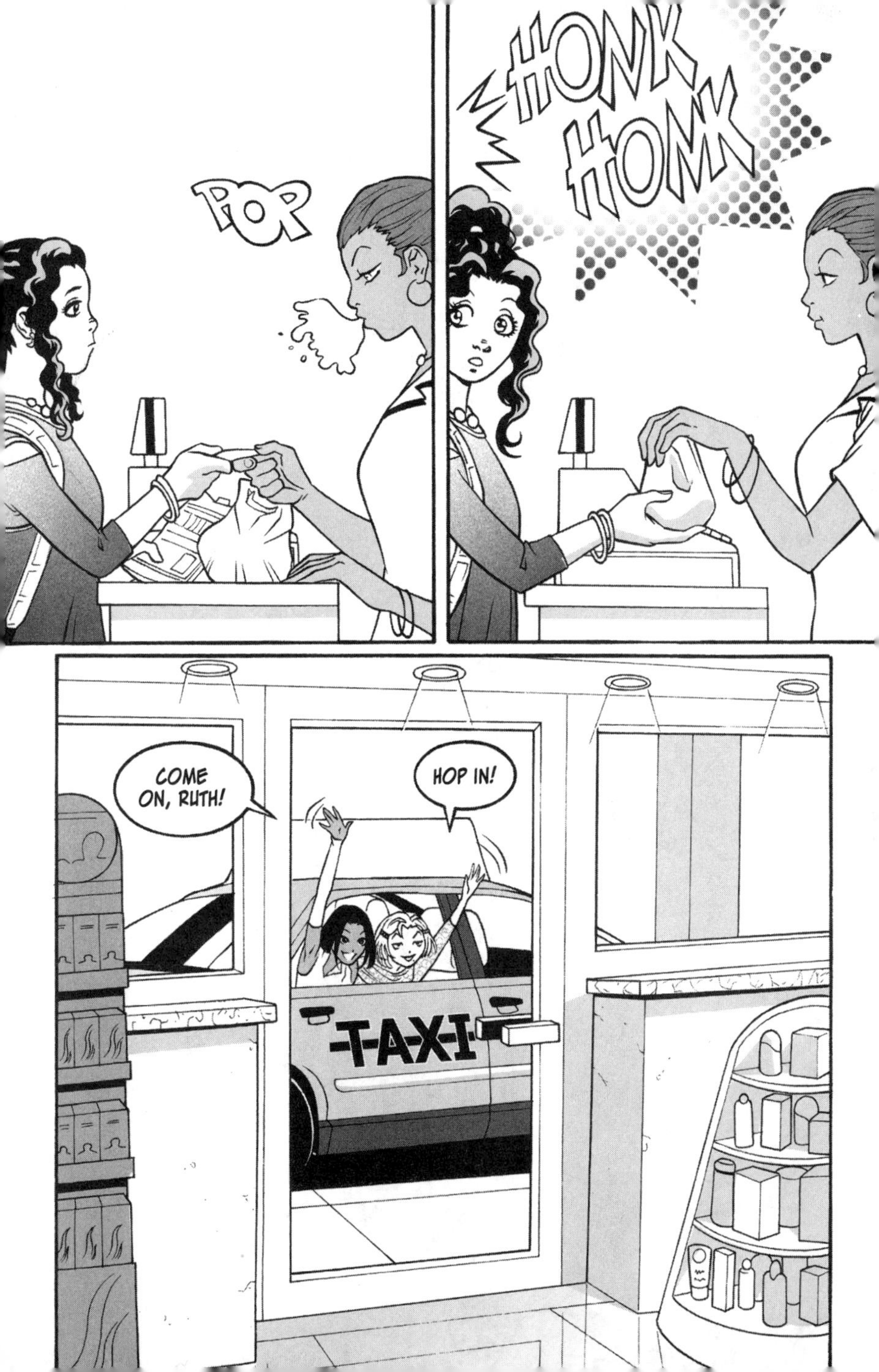
POP
HONK
HONK
COME ON, RUTH!
HOP IN!
TAXI

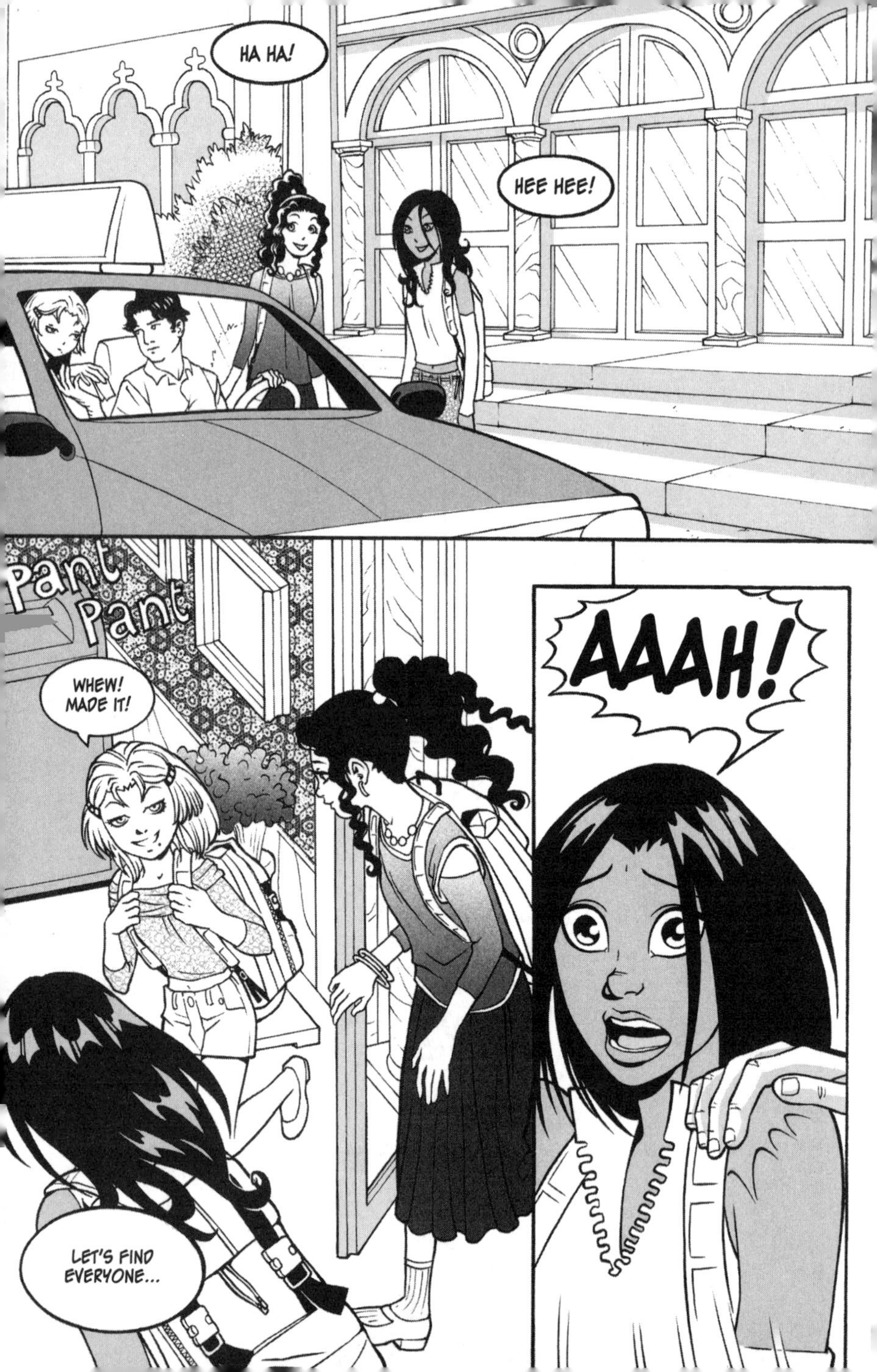
HA HA!
HEE HEE!
Pant Pant
WHEW! MADE IT!
LET'S FIND EVERYONE...
AAAH!

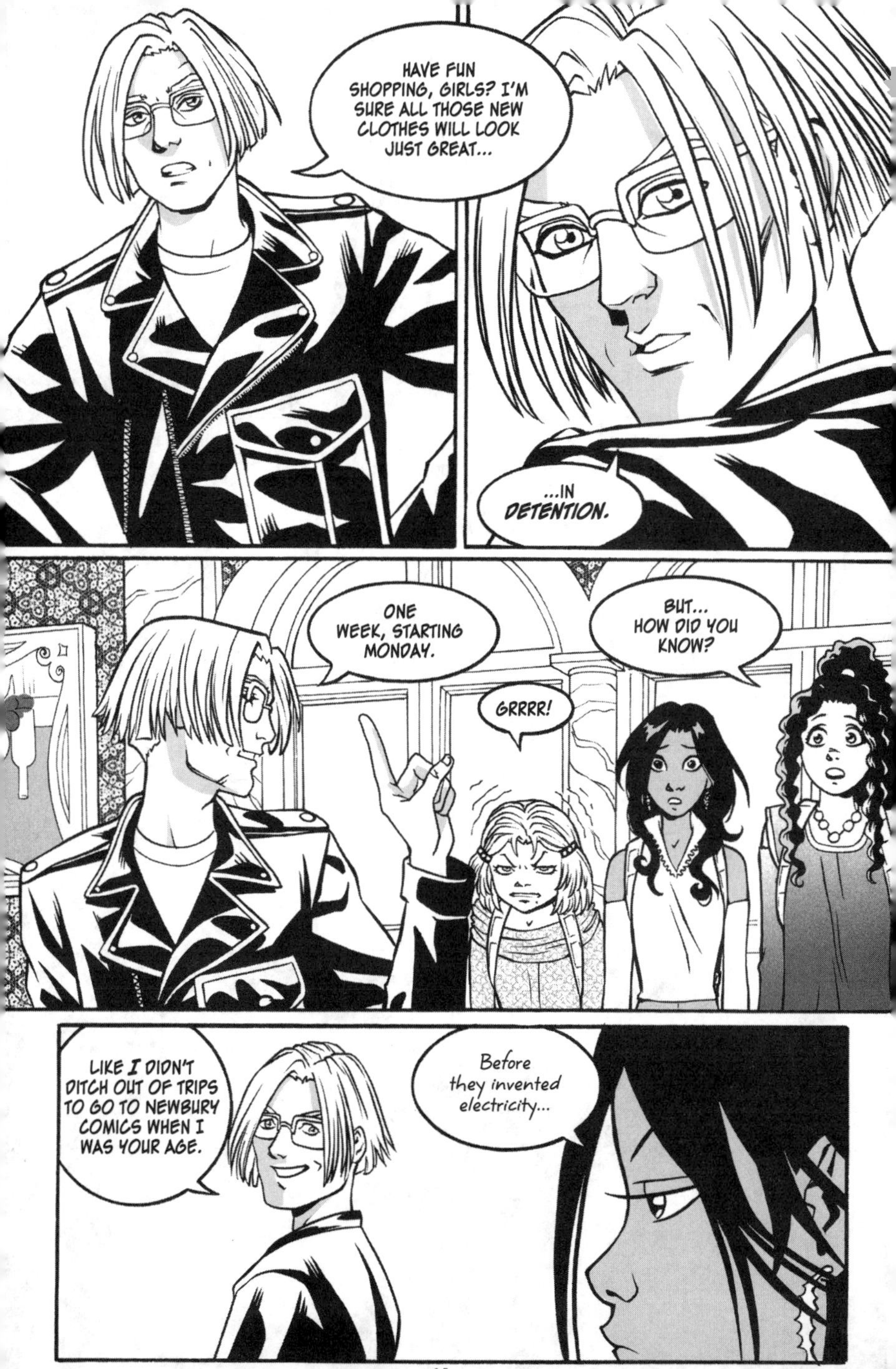
HAVE FUN SHOPPING, GIRLS? I'M SURE ALL THOSE NEW CLOTHES WILL LOOK JUST GREAT...
...IN *DETENTION.*
ONE WEEK, STARTING MONDAY.
GRRRR!
BUT... HOW DID YOU KNOW?
LIKE *I* DIDN'T DITCH OUT OF TRIPS TO GO TO NEWBURY COMICS WHEN I WAS YOUR AGE.
Before they invented electricity...

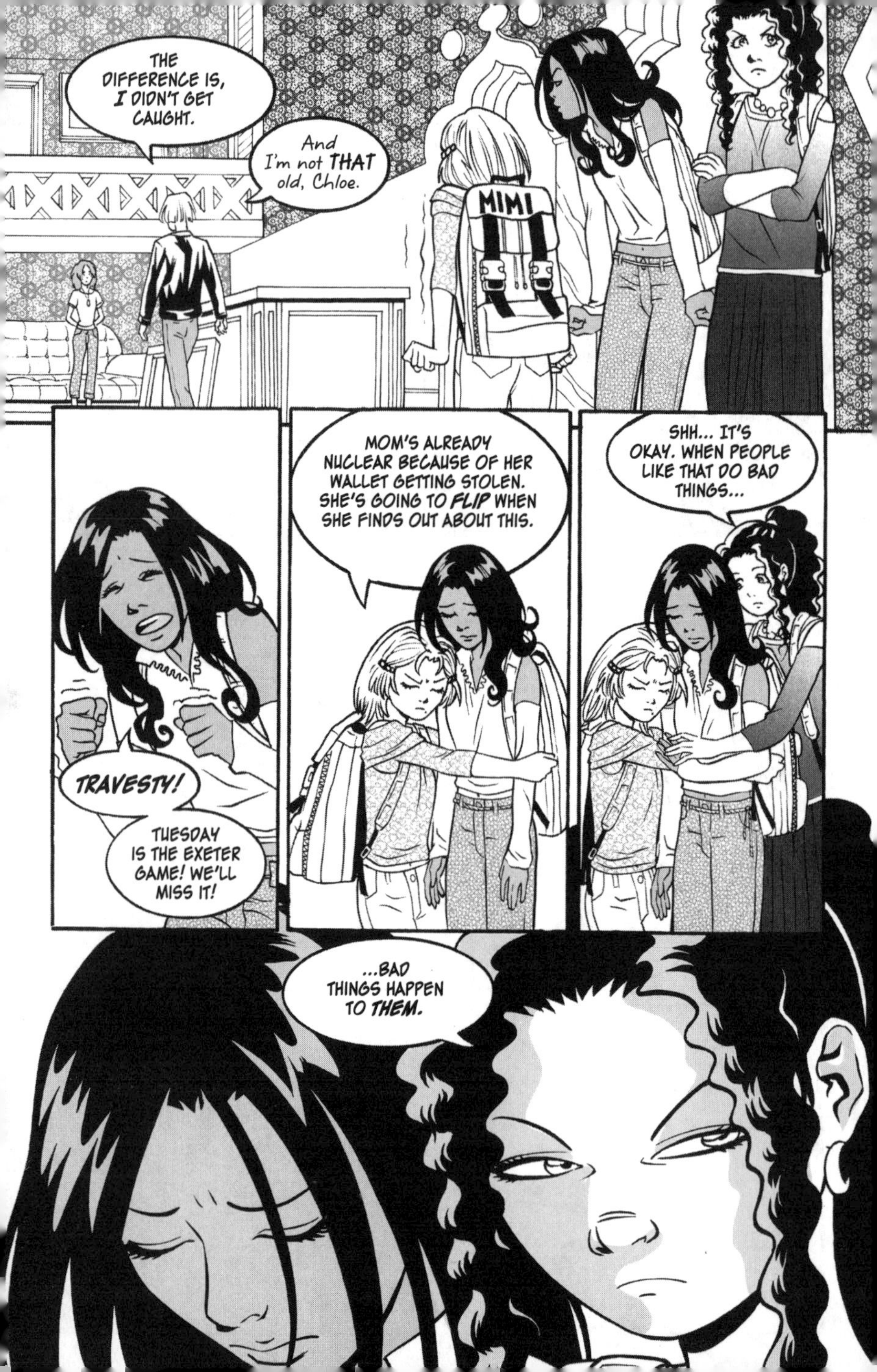
THE DIFFERENCE IS, *I* DIDN'T GET CAUGHT.
And I'm not **THAT** old, Chloe.
TRAVESTY!
TUESDAY IS THE EXETER GAME! WE'LL MISS IT!
MOM'S ALREADY NUCLEAR BECAUSE OF HER WALLET GETTING STOLEN. SHE'S GOING TO *FLIP* WHEN SHE FINDS OUT ABOUT THIS.
SHH... IT'S OKAY. WHEN PEOPLE LIKE THAT DO BAD THINGS...
...BAD THINGS HAPPEN TO *THEM.*

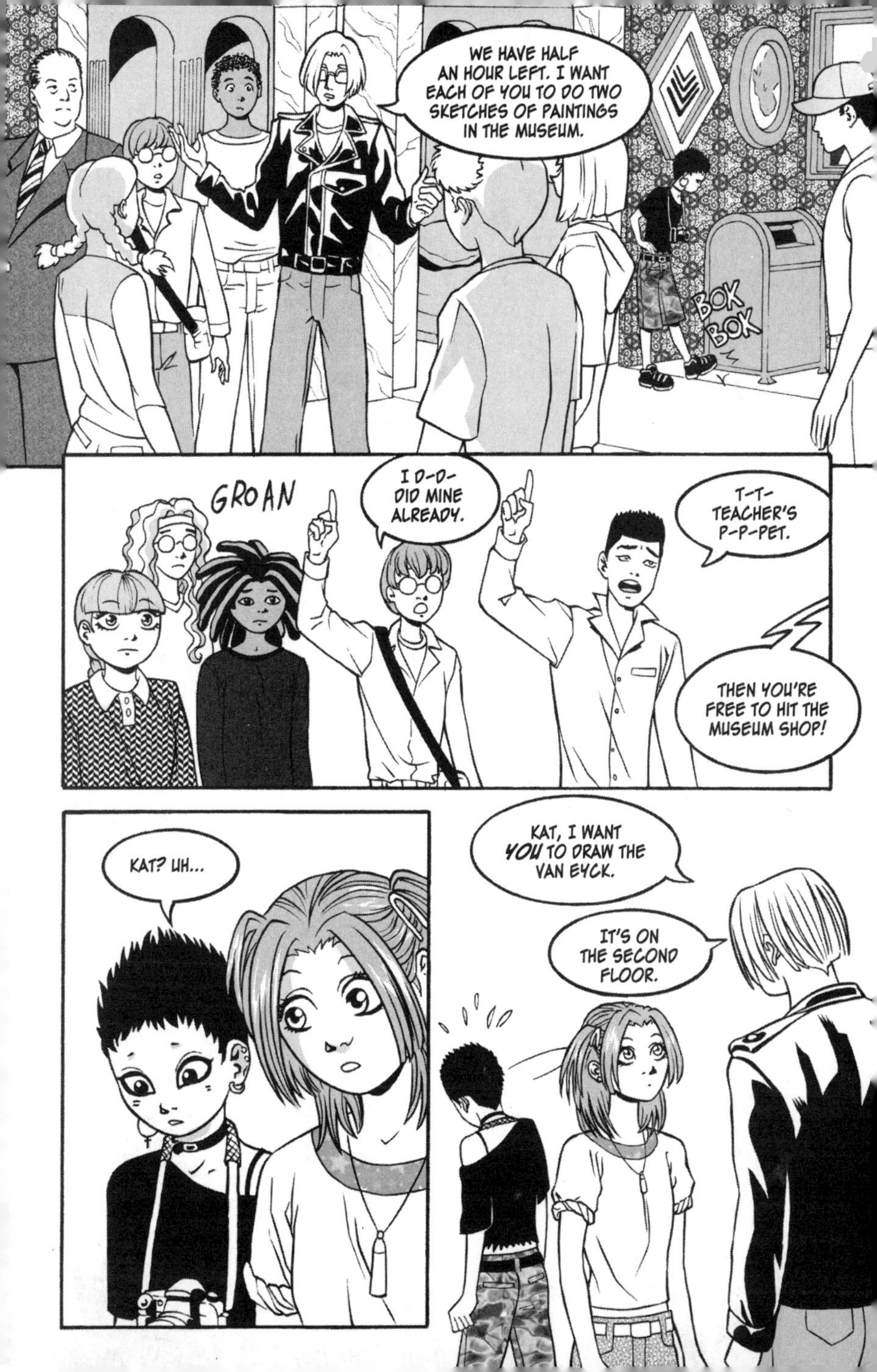

WE HAVE HALF AN HOUR LEFT. I WANT EACH OF YOU TO DO TWO SKETCHES OF PAINTINGS IN THE MUSEUM.
BOK BOK
GROAN
I D-D-DID MINE ALREADY.
T-T-TEACHER'S P-P-PET.
THEN YOU'RE FREE TO HIT THE MUSEUM SHOP!
KAT, I WANT YOU TO DRAW THE VAN EYCK.
IT'S ON THE SECOND FLOOR.
KAT? UH...

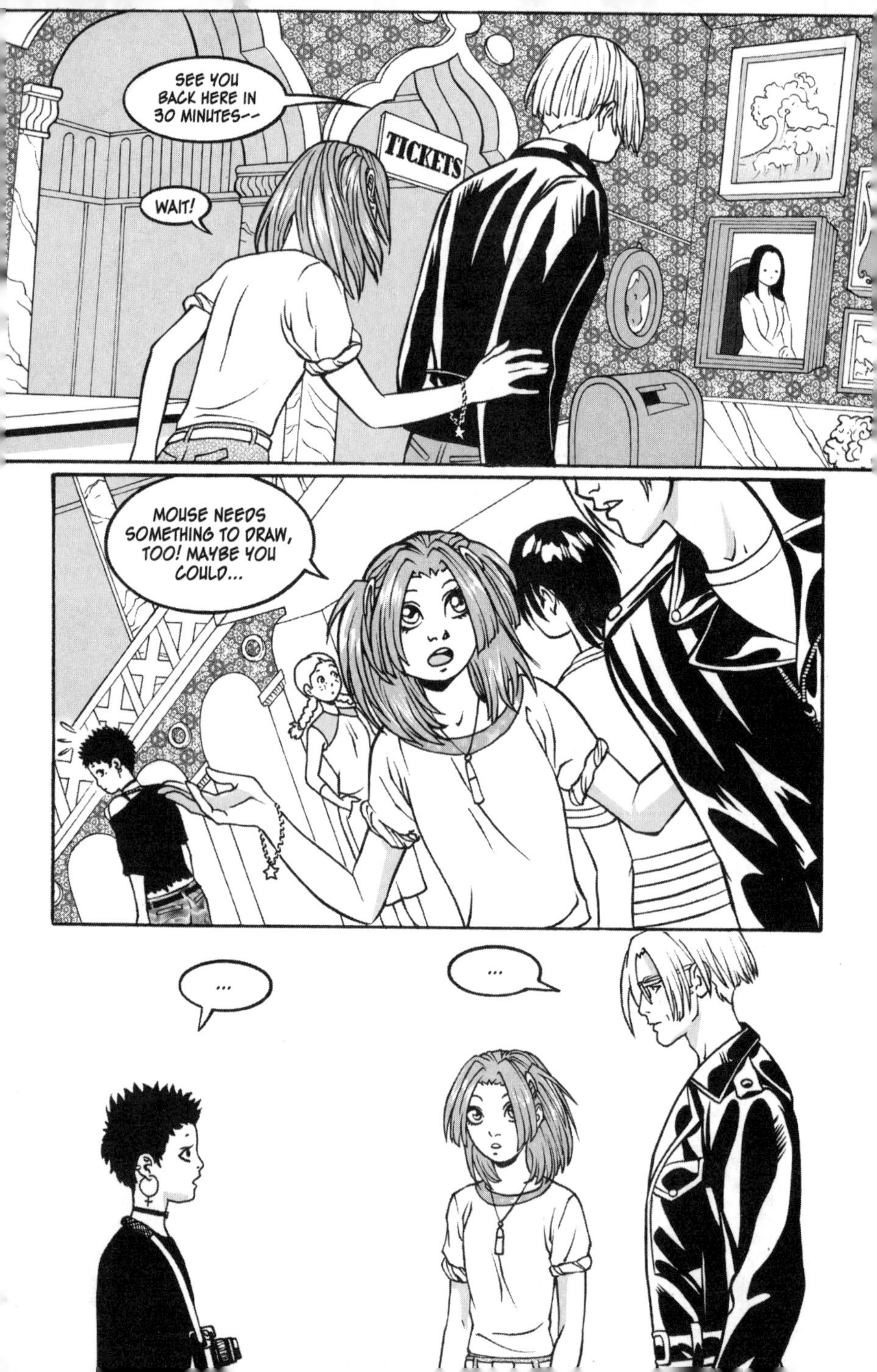
SEE YOU BACK HERE IN 30 MINUTES--
TICKETS
WAIT!
MOUSE NEEDS SOMETHING TO DRAW, TOO! MAYBE YOU COULD...
...
...

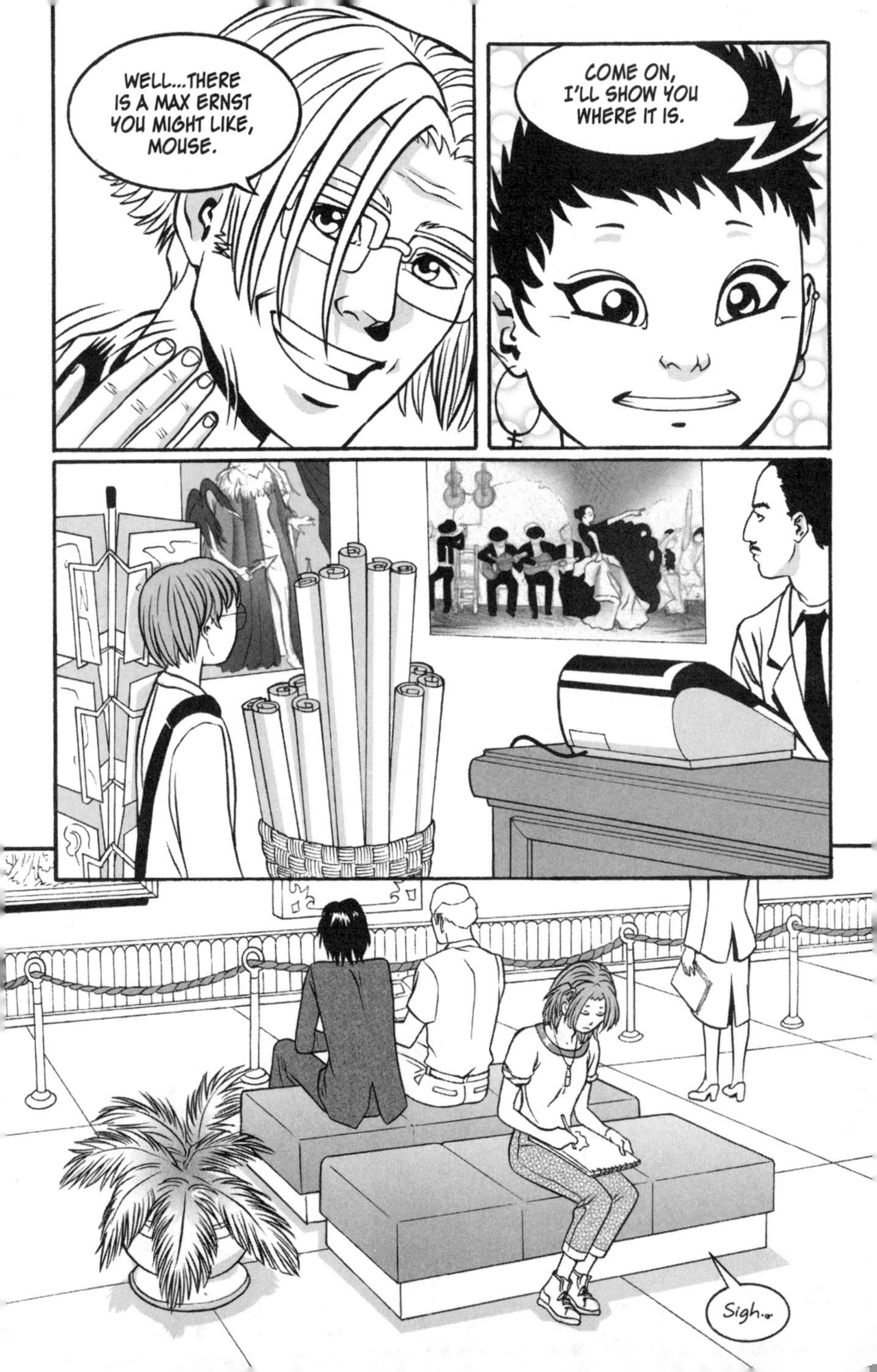
WELL...THERE IS A MAX ERNST YOU MIGHT LIKE, MOUSE.
COME ON, I'LL SHOW YOU WHERE IT IS.
Sigh...

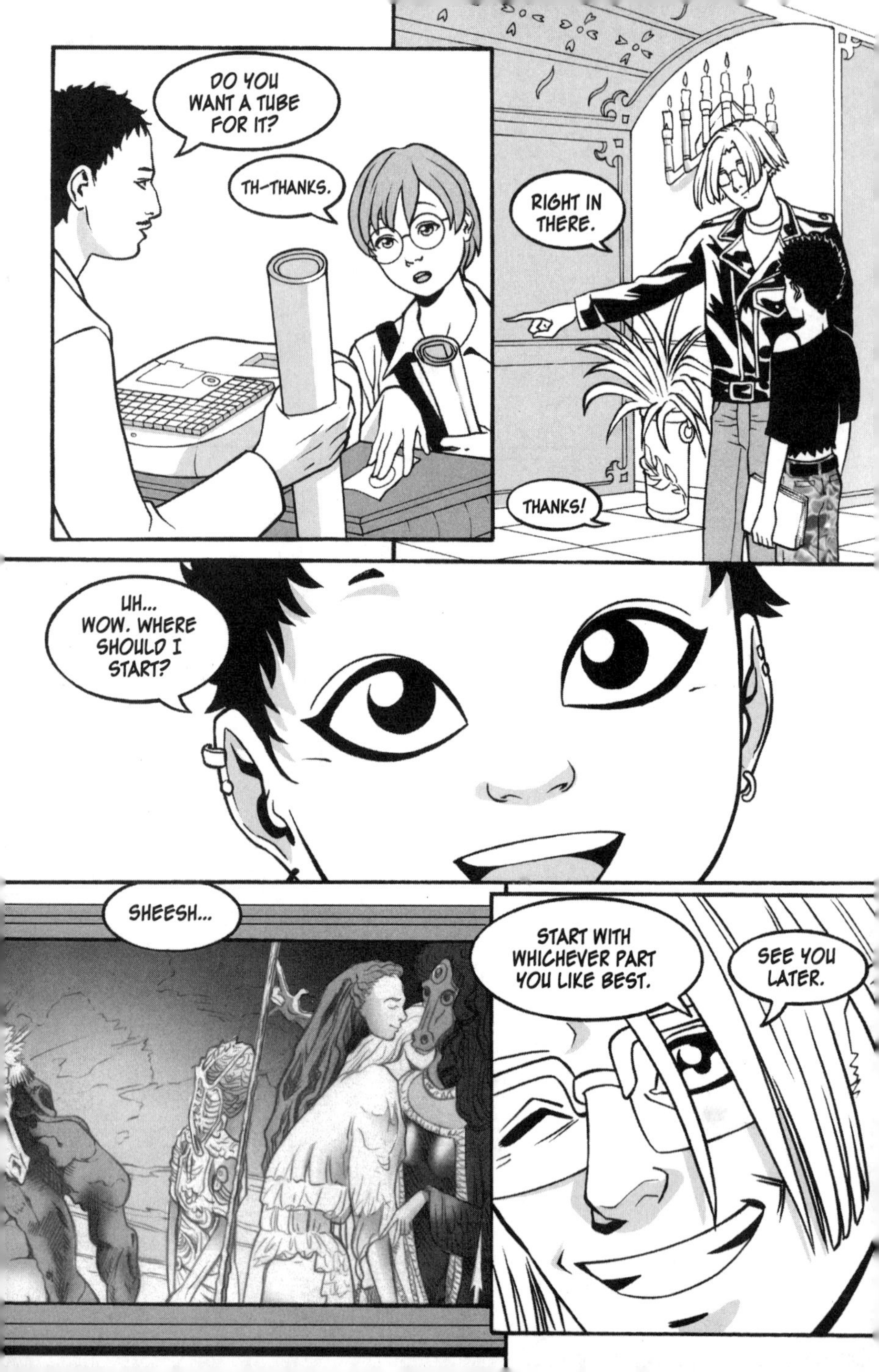
DO YOU WANT A TUBE FOR IT?
TH-THANKS.
RIGHT IN THERE.
THANKS!
UH... WOW. WHERE SHOULD I START?
SHEESH...
START WITH WHICHEVER PART YOU LIKE BEST.
SEE YOU LATER.

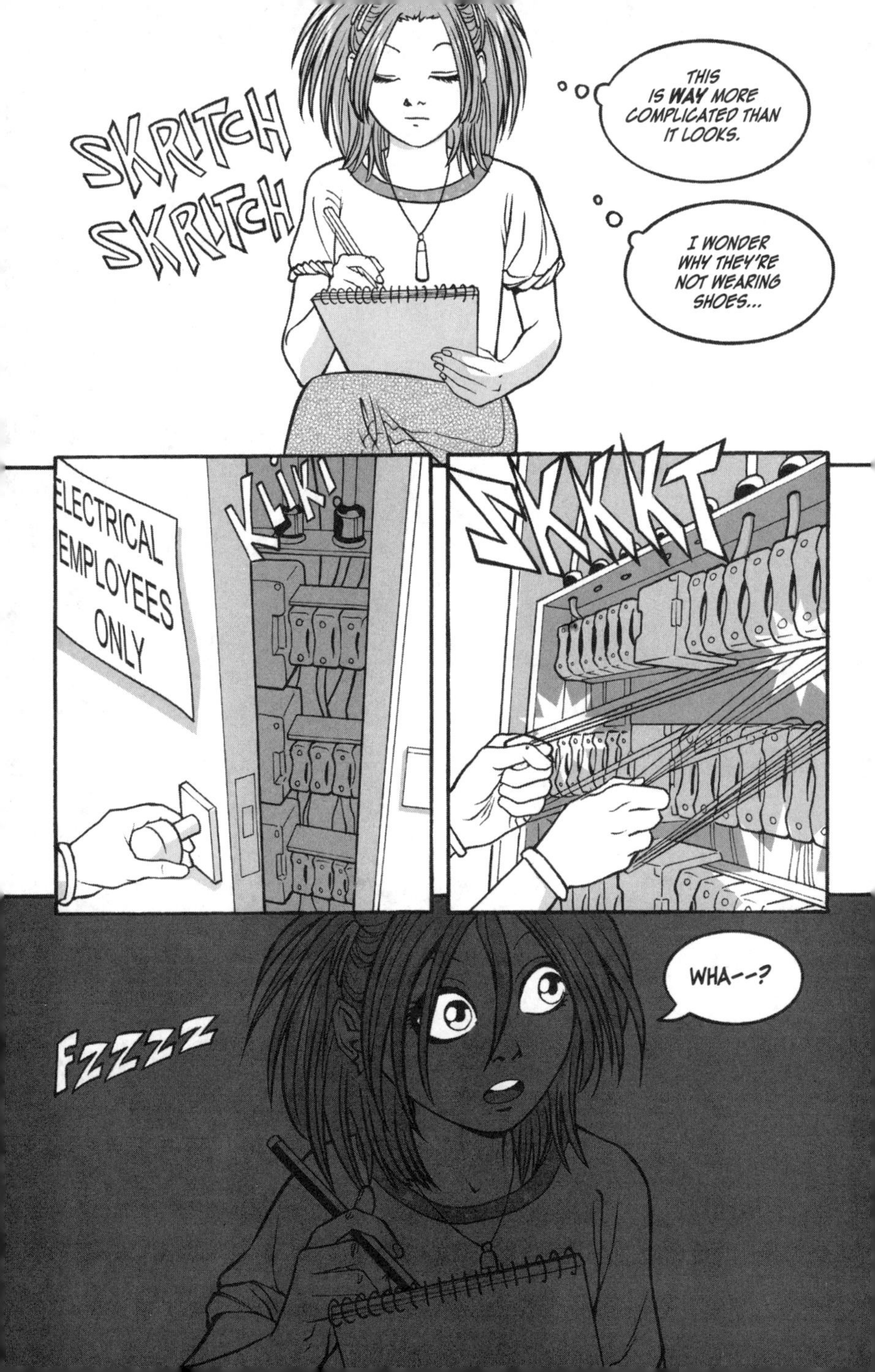
SKRITCH SKRITCH
THIS IS WAY MORE COMPLICATED THAN IT LOOKS.
I WONDER WHY THEY'RE NOT WEARING SHOES...
ELECTRICAL EMPLOYEES ONLY
KLIK
SKKKT
WHA--?
FZZZZ

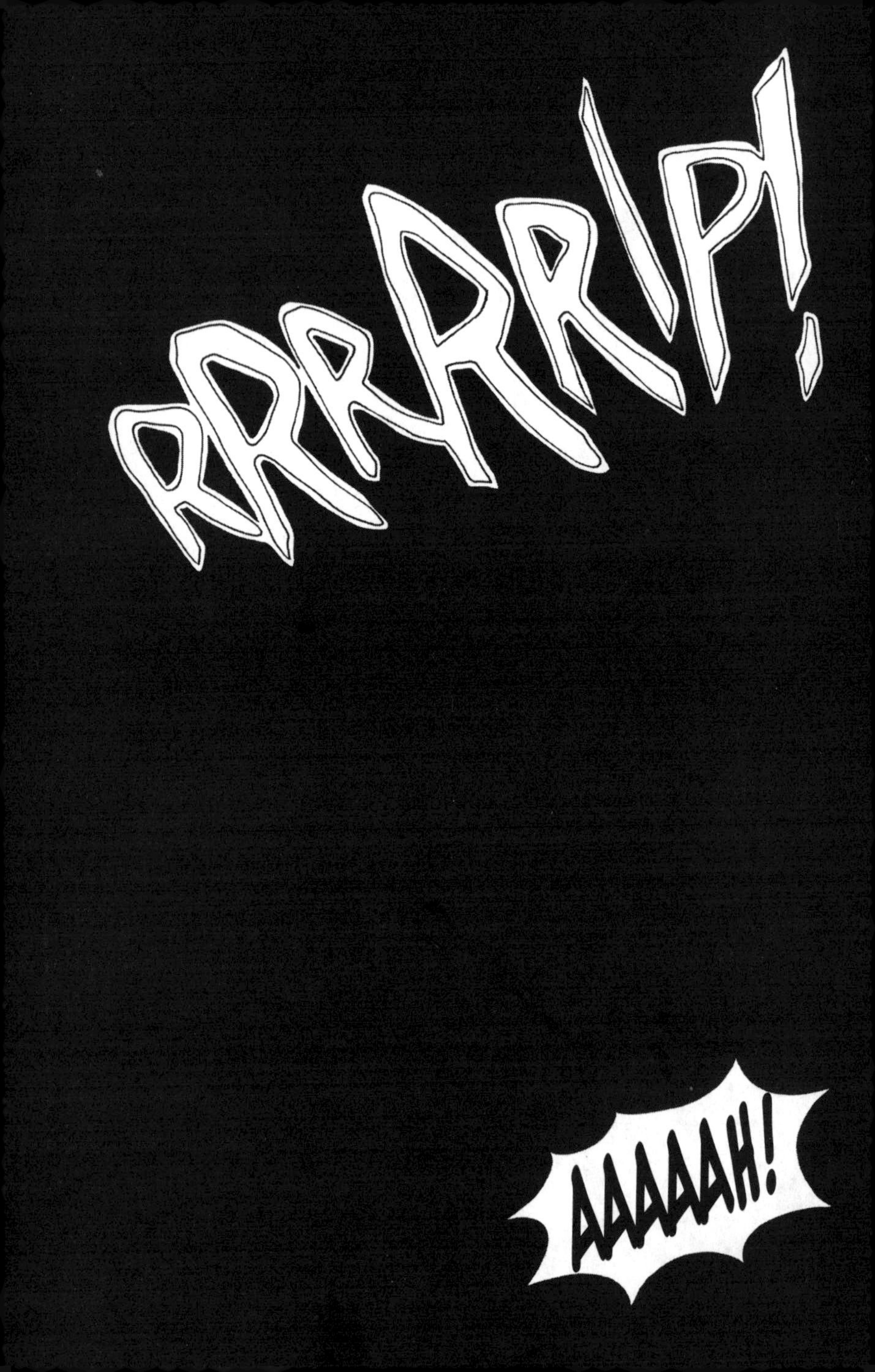
RRRRRIP!
AAAAAH!

Chapter 4:
The Spanish Prisoner

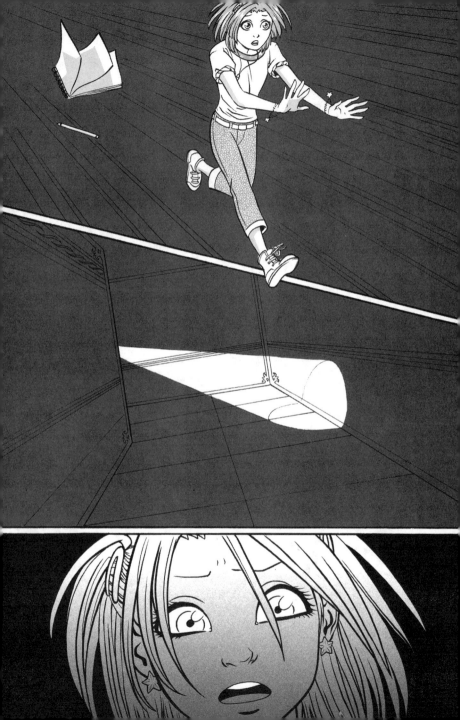

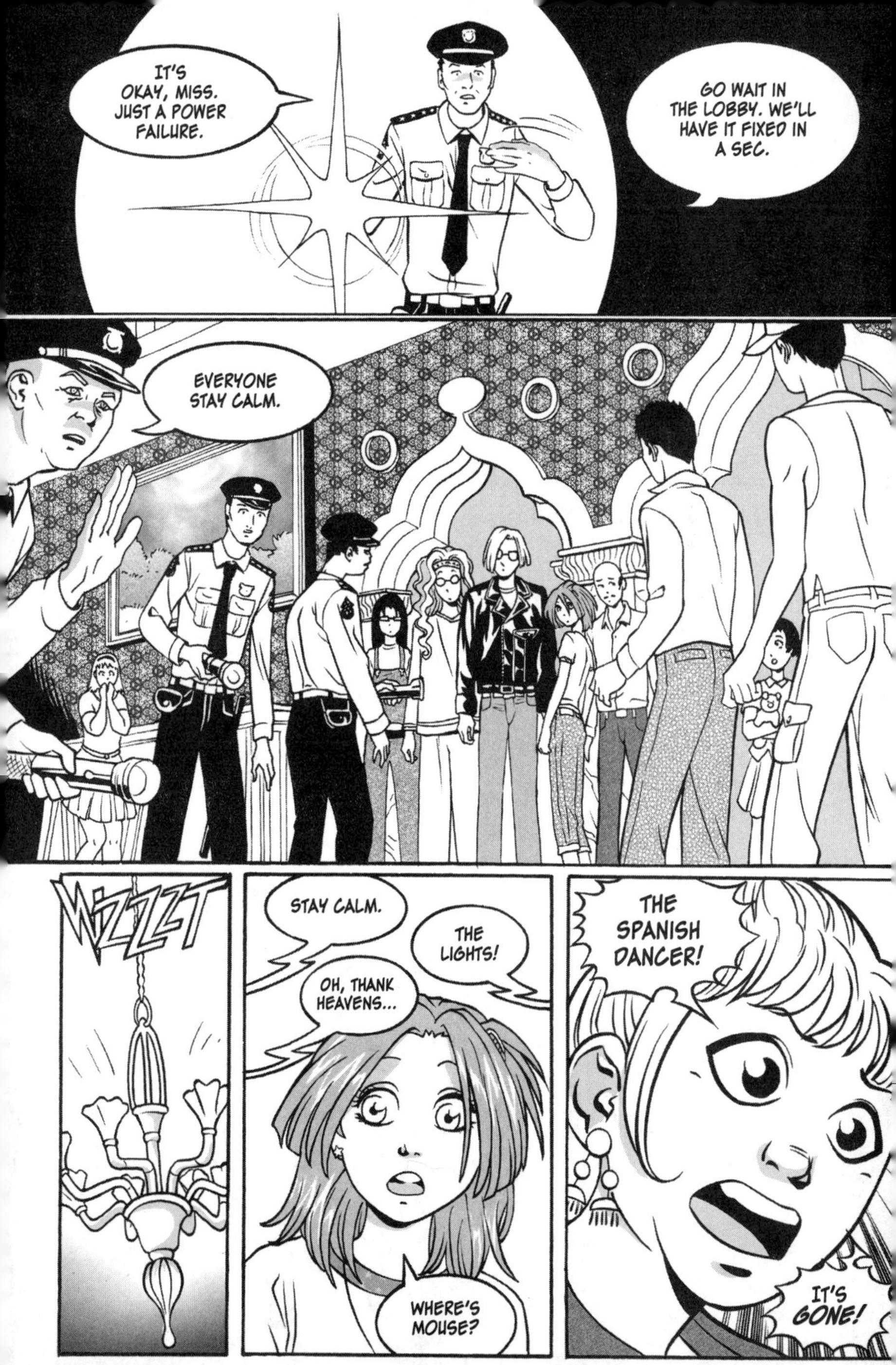
IT'S OKAY, MISS. JUST A POWER FAILURE.
GO WAIT IN THE LOBBY. WE'LL HAVE IT FIXED IN A SEC.
EVERYONE STAY CALM.
WIZZZT
STAY CALM.
THE LIGHTS!
OH, THANK HEAVENS...
WHERE'S MOUSE?
THE SPANISH DANCER!
IT'S GONE!

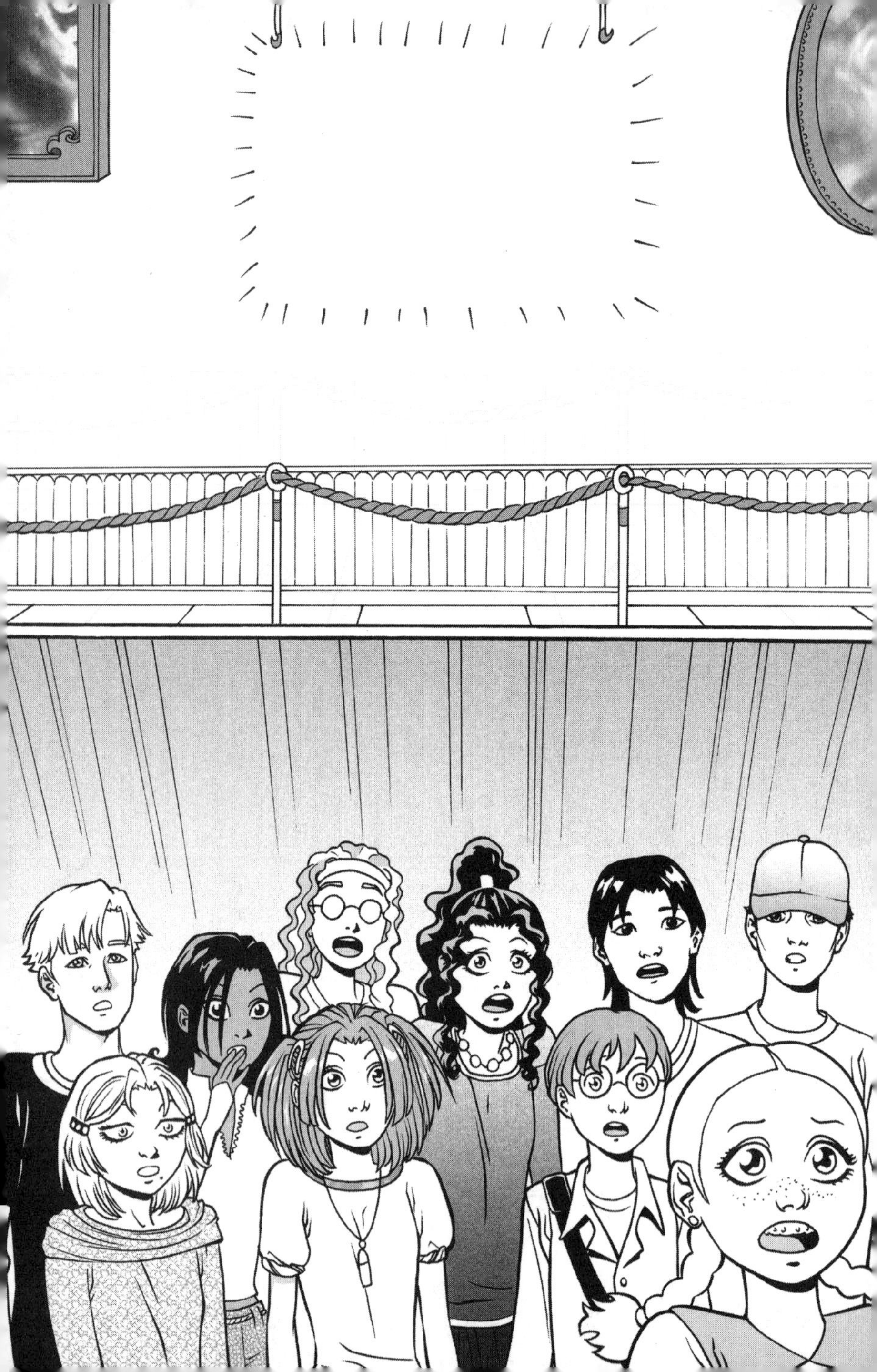

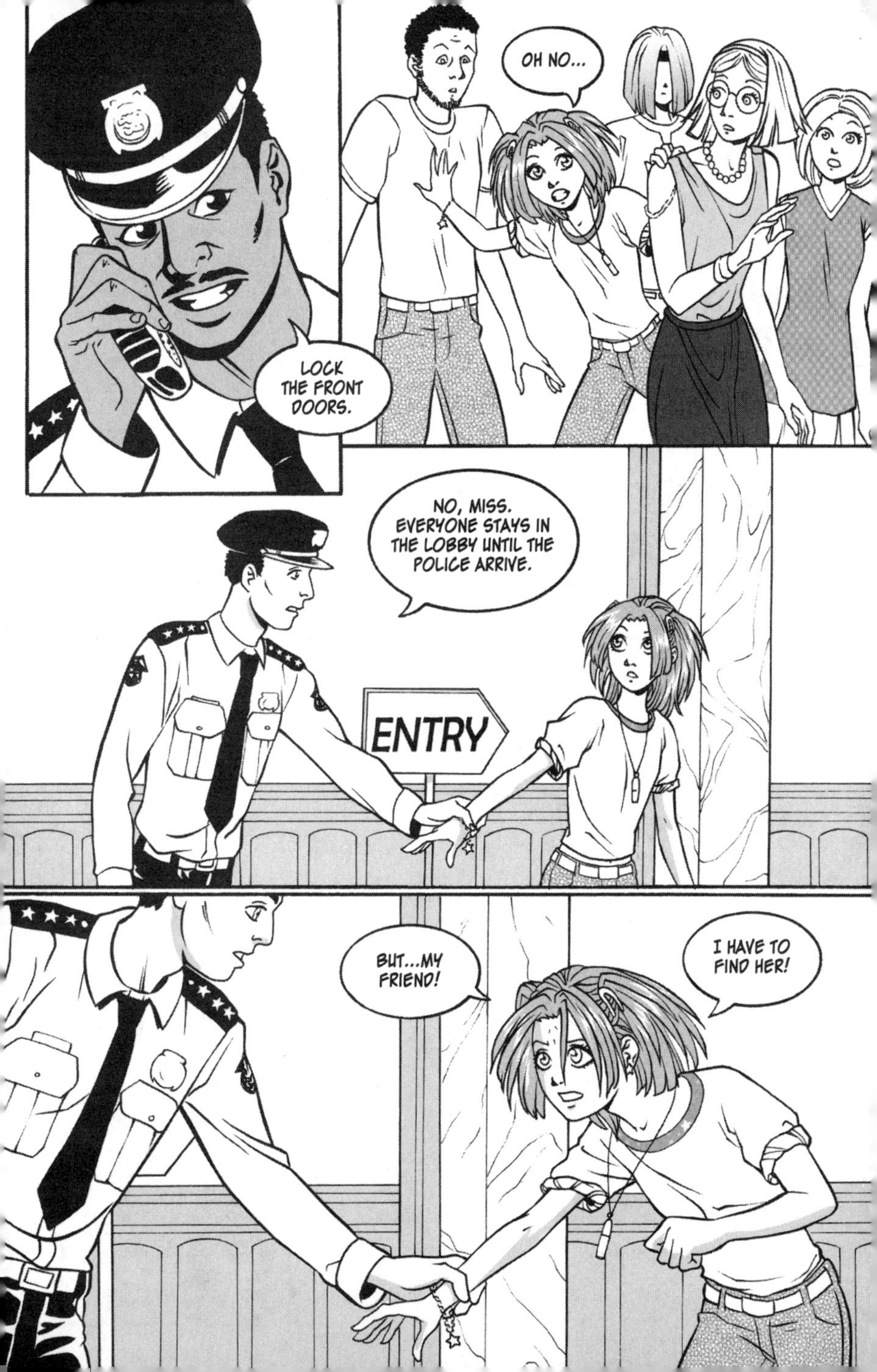
LOCK THE FRONT DOORS.
OH NO...
NO, MISS. EVERYONE STAYS IN THE LOBBY UNTIL THE POLICE ARRIVE.
ENTRY
BUT...MY FRIEND!
I HAVE TO FIND HER!

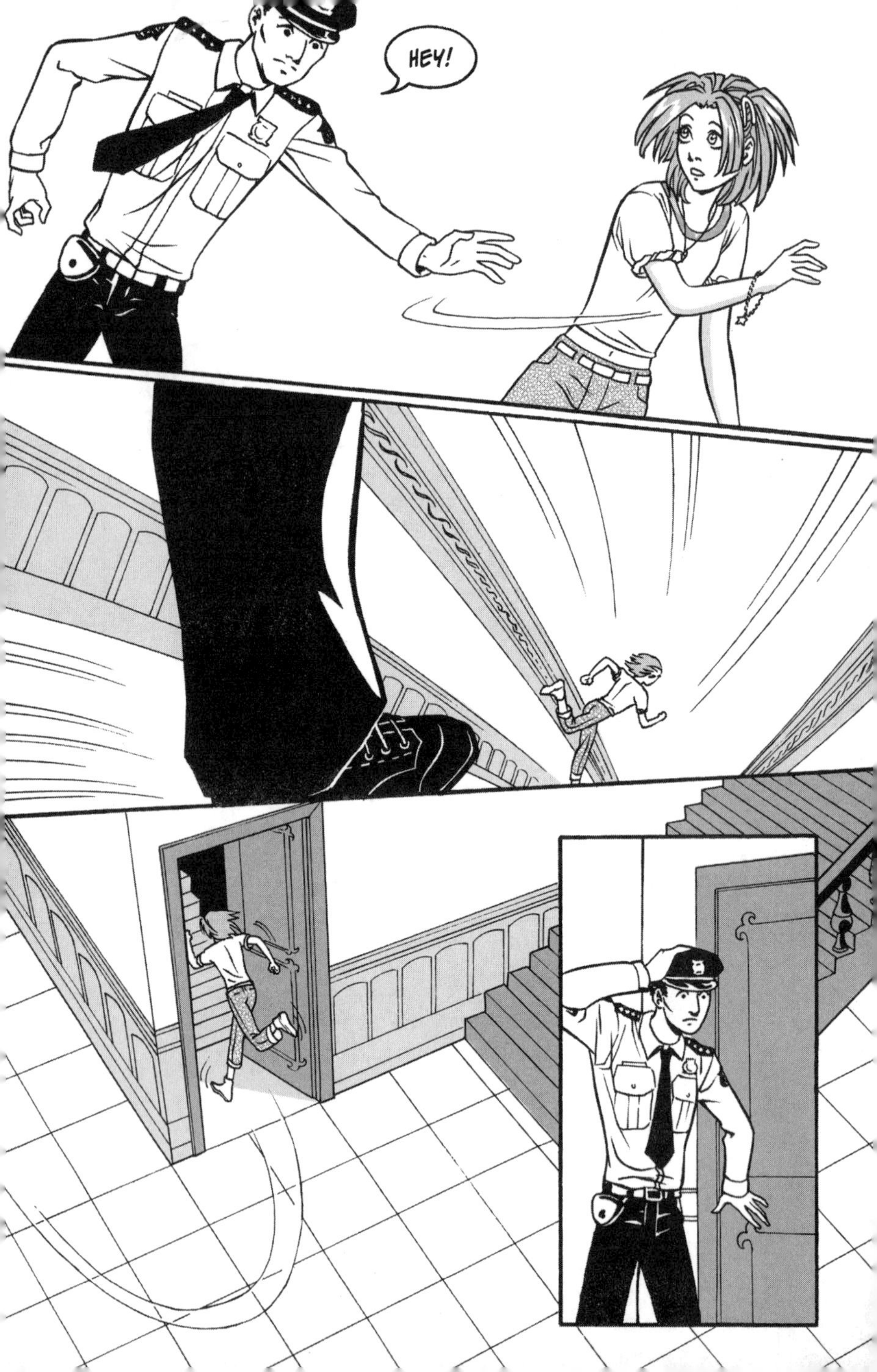
HEY!

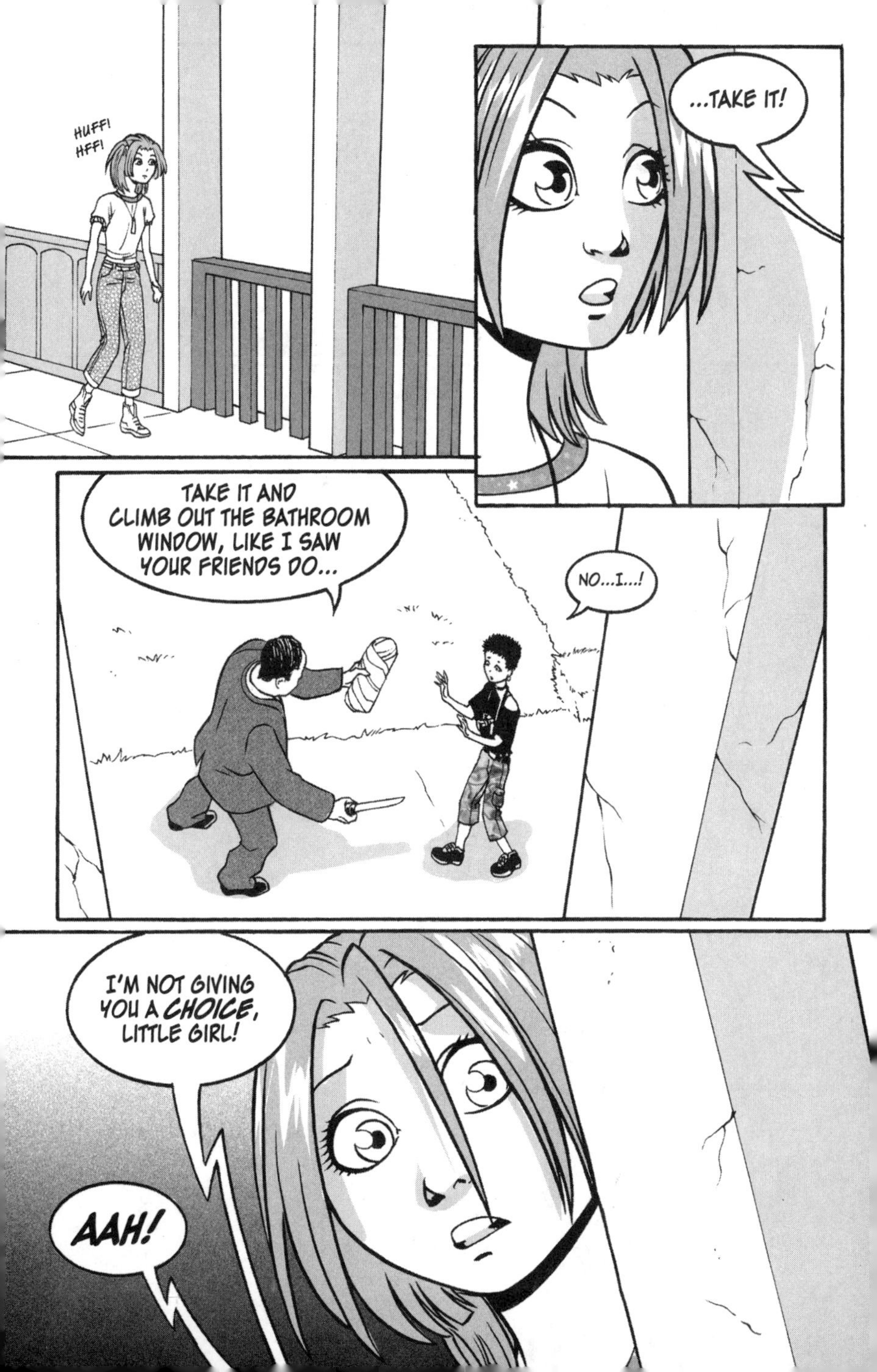
HUFF! HFF!
...TAKE IT!
TAKE IT AND CLIMB OUT THE BATHROOM WINDOW, LIKE I SAW YOUR FRIENDS DO...
NO...I...!
I'M NOT GIVING YOU A *CHOICE*, LITTLE GIRL!
AAH!

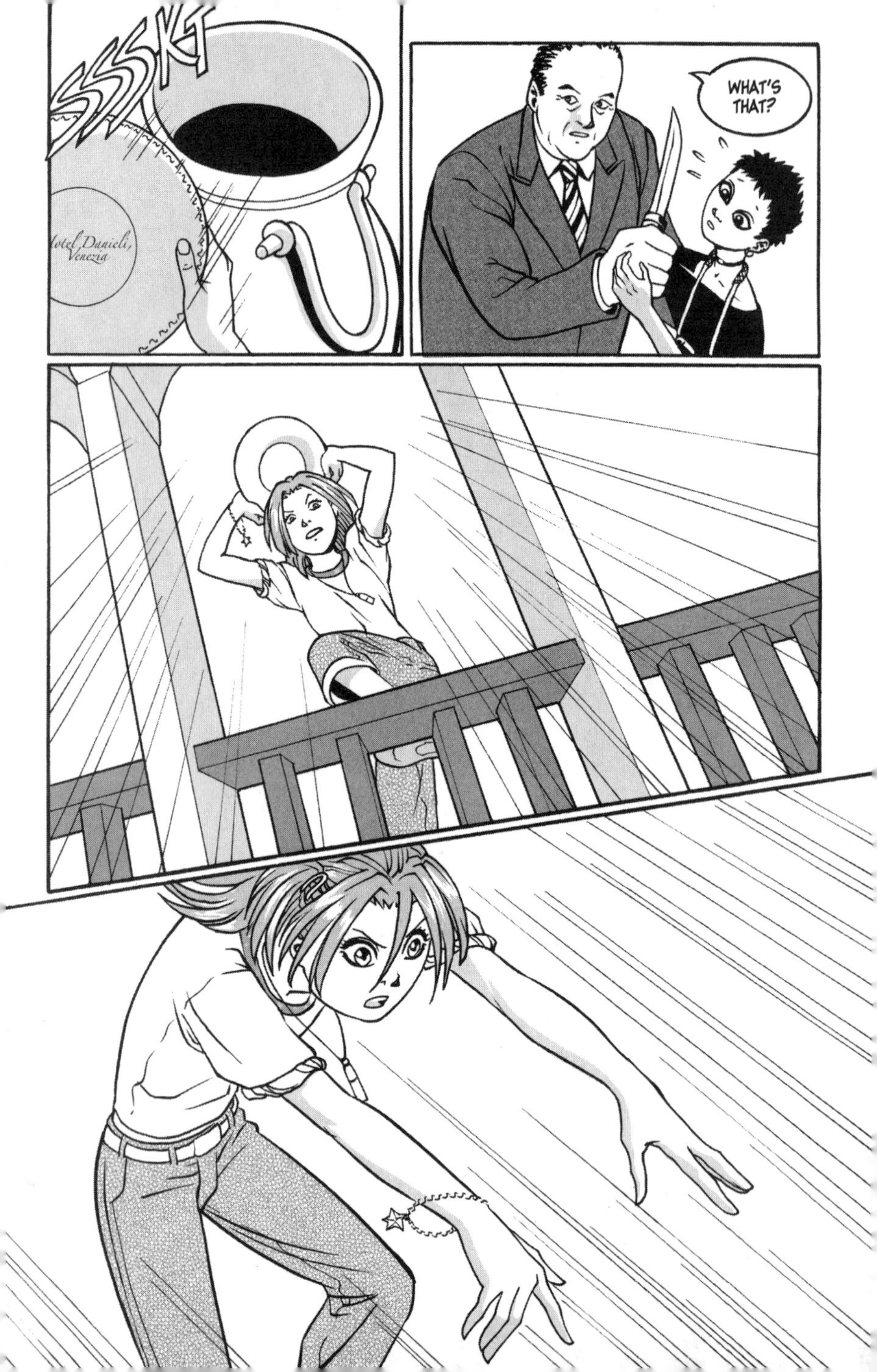
SSSKT
Hotel Danieli, Venezia
WHAT'S THAT?

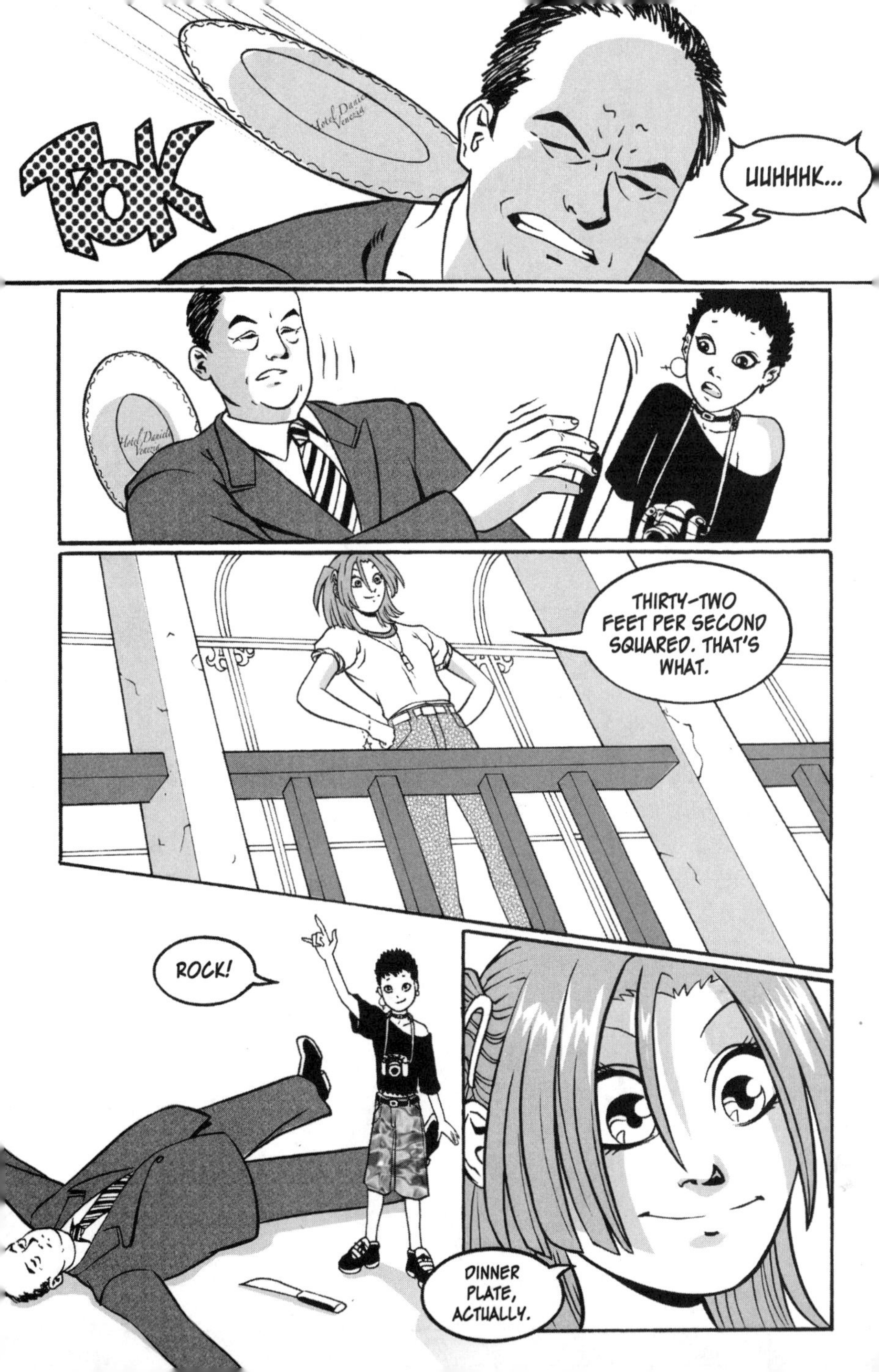
TOK
UUHHHK...
Hotel Danieli Venezia
THIRTY-TWO FEET PER SECOND SQUARED. THAT'S WHAT.
ROCK!
DINNER PLATE, ACTUALLY.

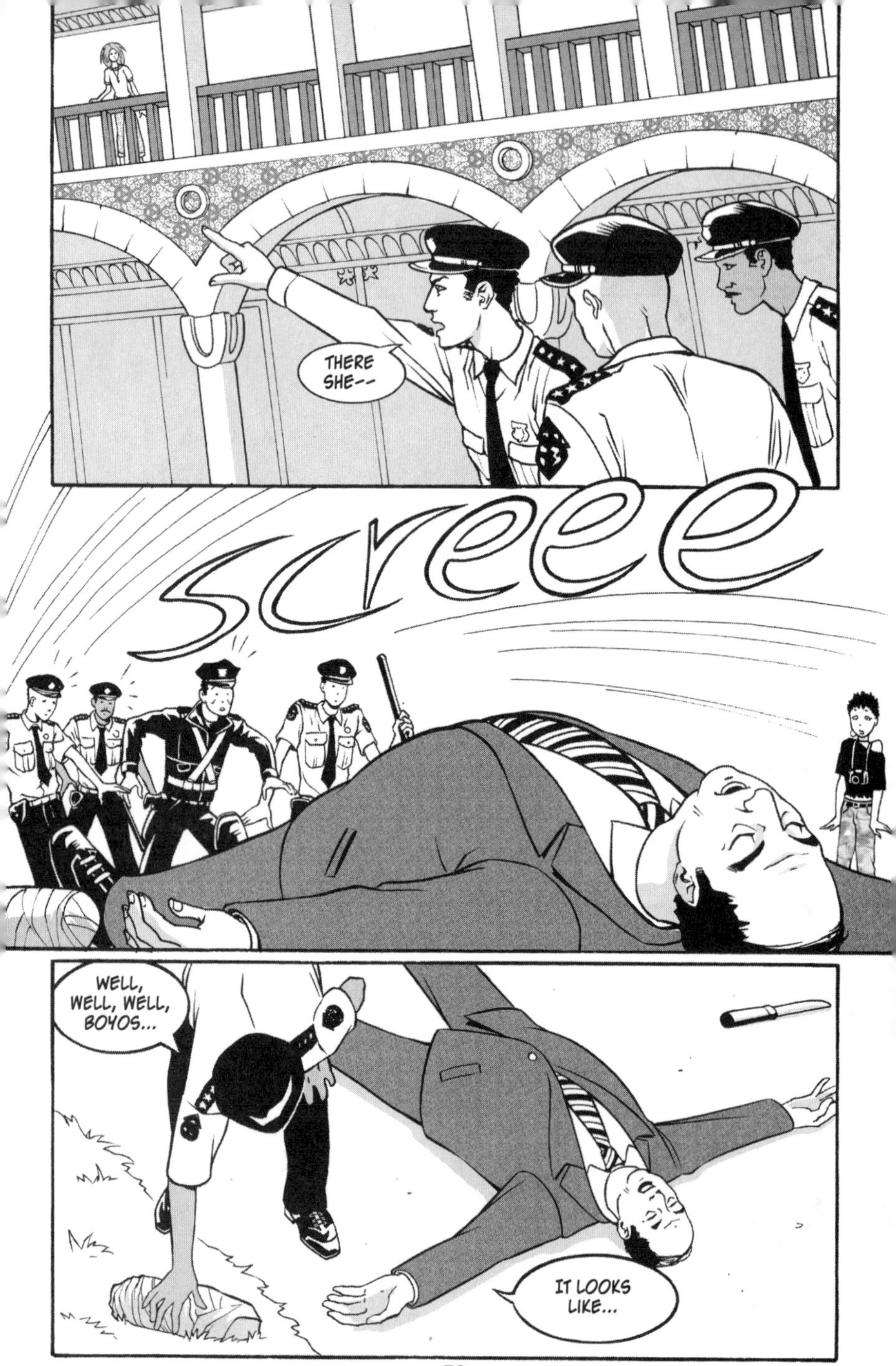
THERE SHE--
SCREEE
WELL, WELL, WELL, BOYOS...
IT LOOKS LIKE...

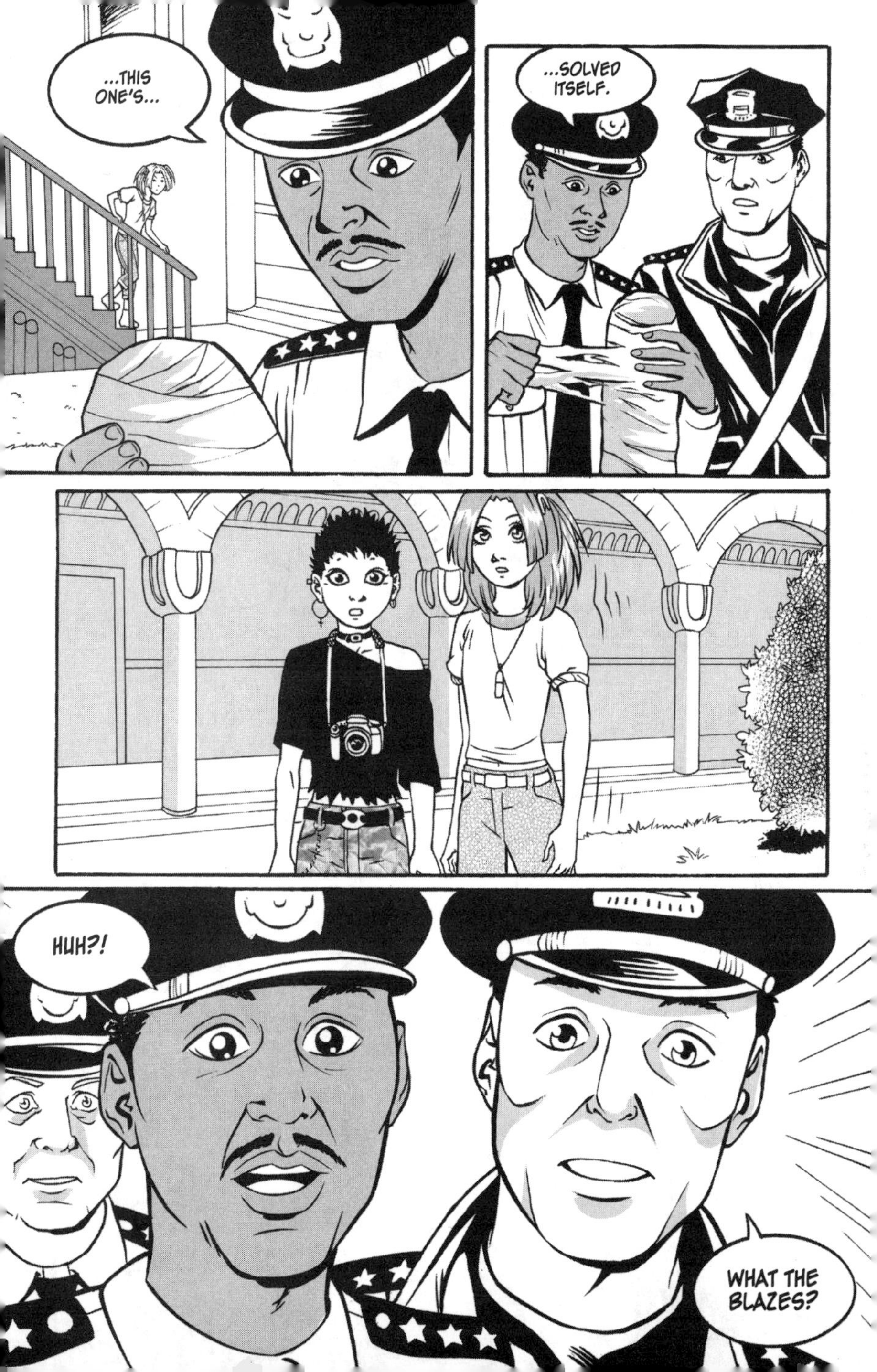
...THIS ONE'S...
...SOLVED ITSELF.
HUH?!
WHAT THE BLAZES?

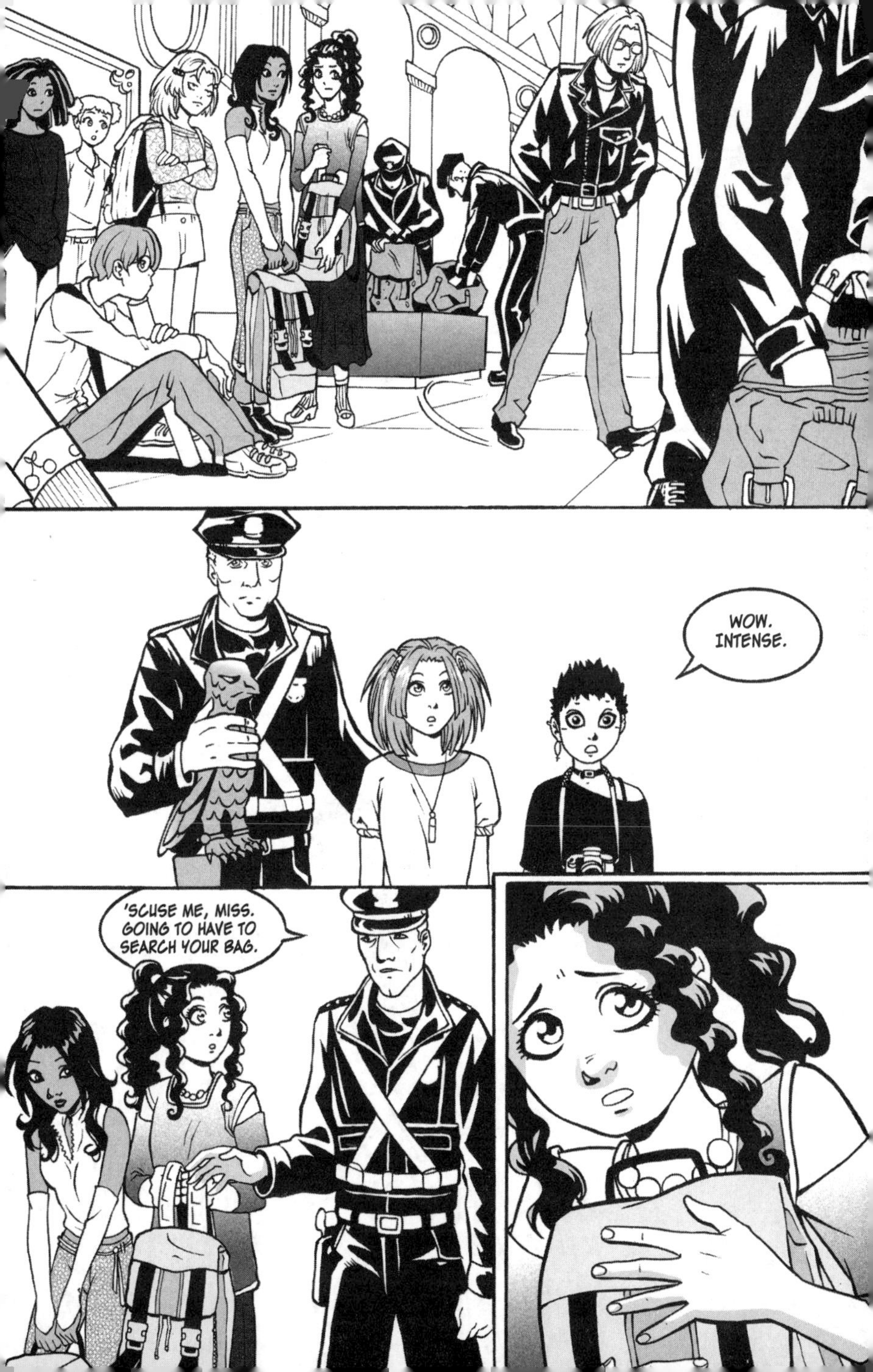
WOW. INTENSE.
'SCUSE ME, MISS. GOING TO HAVE TO SEARCH YOUR BAG.

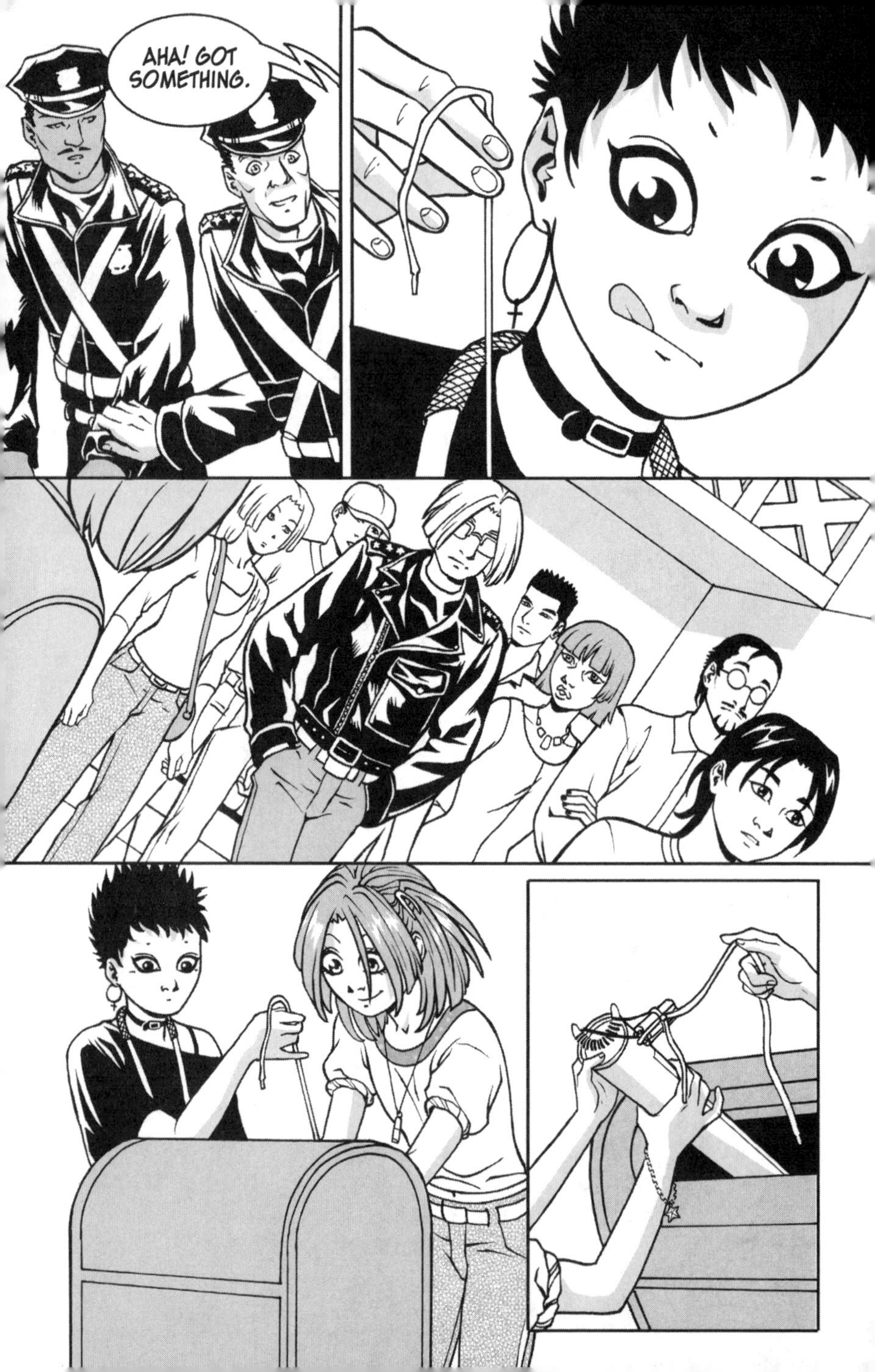
AHA! GOT SOMETHING.

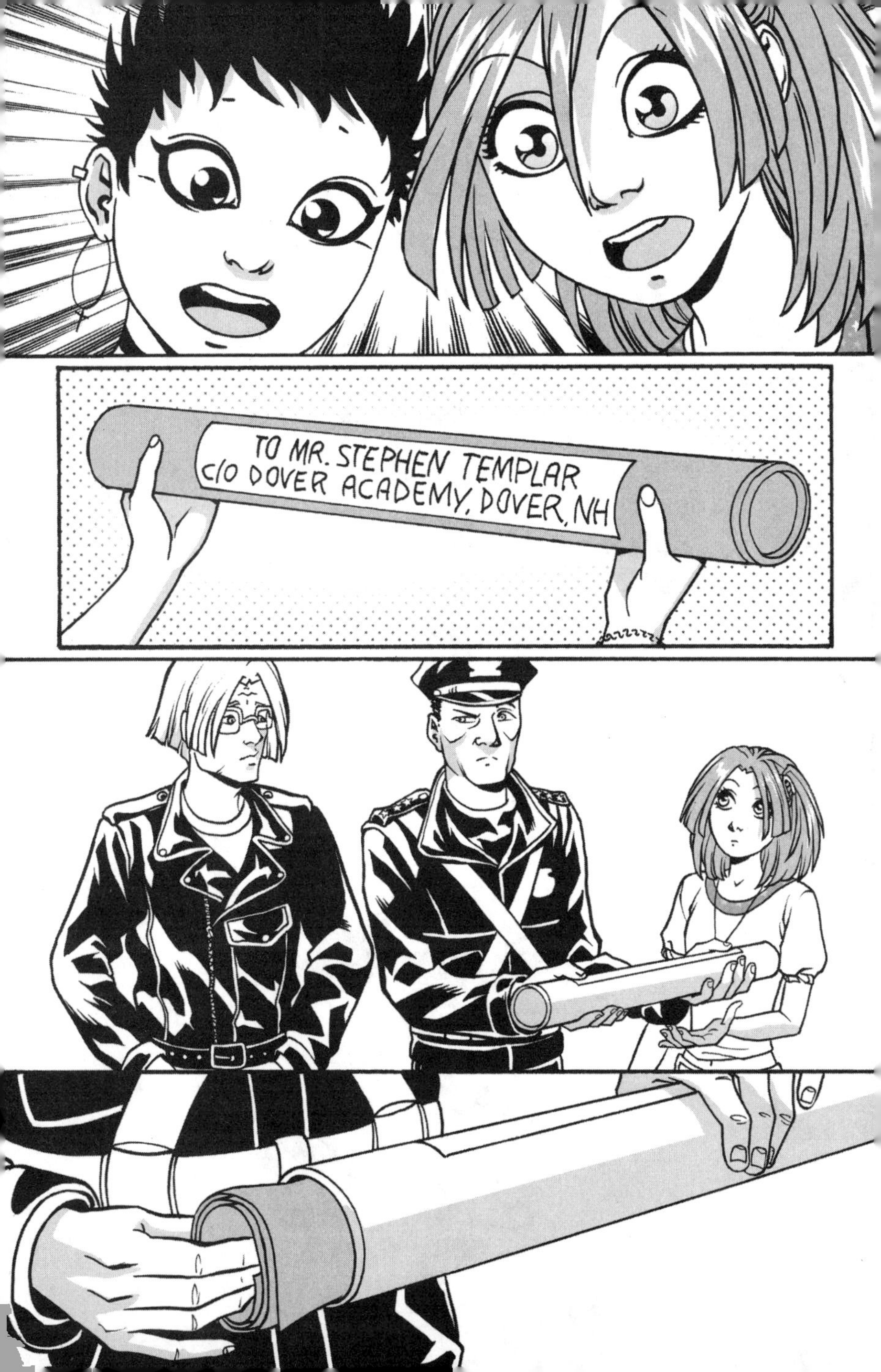
TO MR. STEPHEN TEMPLAR
C/O DOVER ACADEMY, DOVER, NH

Try This at Home!

Want to make your own electromagnet the way Kat & Mouse do in Chapter 4? Here's how!

You'll need:
- A big iron nail, about six inches long
- Insulated copper wire, about 12 feet
- A D-cell battery
- A pair of wire strippers
- Some metal paperclips
- A little bit of duct tape
- A parent nearby

You should be able to find most of these things at your local hardware store.

Wrap the wire around the nail. The more (and the tighter) you wrap it, the stronger your electromagnet will be. Leave about a foot of wire at each end.

Strip off about an inch of the plastic insulation from each end of the wire. Tape one end of the bare copper wire to the top of the D-cell battery, and the other end to the bottom of the battery.

Now, empty the paperclips onto a smooth surface. Hold your nail near the paperclips. One end should push the paperclips away, and the other end should pick them up.

How does it work? Every electric current produces a magnetic field. Usually, this is so small that you can't feel it — that's why the paperclips won't move if you just put the wire near them. But by wrapping the wire in loops around the nail, you've concentrated the magnetic field so it becomes more powerful. The more loops, the more power in the magnetic field.

Where does the electric current come from? Well, when you attach one end of the wire to the positive terminal of the battery, and the other end to the negative terminal, the electrons go streaming from the negative side of the battery through the wire to the positive side. That's an electric current! As the iron nail is not naturally magnetic, if you take the current away, you have no magnet.

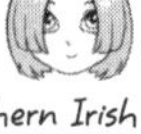

KAT'S HEROES 2: JOCELYN BELL BURNELL

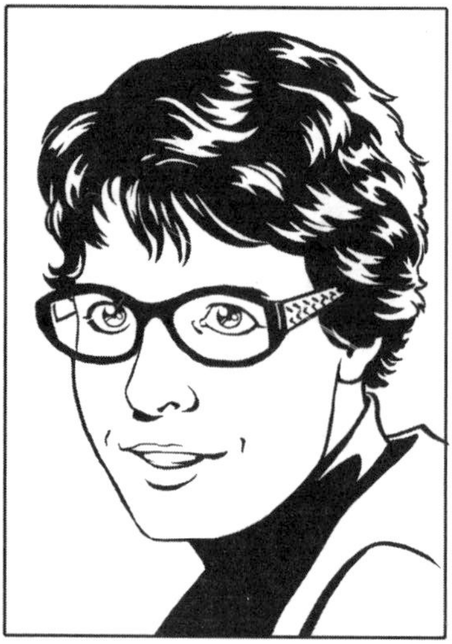

Northern Irish astrophysicist Jocelyn Bell Burnell flunked her high school entrance exams when she was 11, making it difficult for her to get a coveted spot in Britain's school system. As a result, her parents sent her to a private boarding school in England, which, by chance, had a fantastic physics teacher. Jocelyn was inspired, and went on to study physics at college, and eventually got accepted into the world-famous Cambridge University to do graduate work in physics.

Jocelyn's PhD work was helping her professor, Anthony Hewish, in building a gigantic radio telescope to study quasars: massive, irregular sources of electromagnetic energy in space. As Jocelyn was examining miles of printouts, she noticed some radio signals that were too fast and too regular for quasars. After analysis, she determined that these signals must come from rapidly spinning, super-dense, collapsed stars: pulsars. She and Anthony named the first one "LGM-1", for "Little Green Men" (since they had first joked that the signals were aliens radioing them from space.)

Anthony got a Nobel Prize for the pulsar discovery, but Jocelyn was famously, and controversially, left out. However, Jocelyn went on to teach and hold research positions at many universities, including Princeton and Oxford. She was also president of the Royal Astronomical Society.

Not bad for someone who was a "failure" at school!

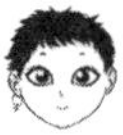

MOUSE'S HEROES 2: AMELIA EARHART

Amelia Earhart first decided she wanted to fly after attending a stunt-flying exhibition when she was 20. She worked as a social worker to save up enough money to buy her first airplane: a second-hand two-seater biplane that was painted bright yellow. Amelia named it "Canary", and set her first women's record with it: flying to a height of 14,000 feet.

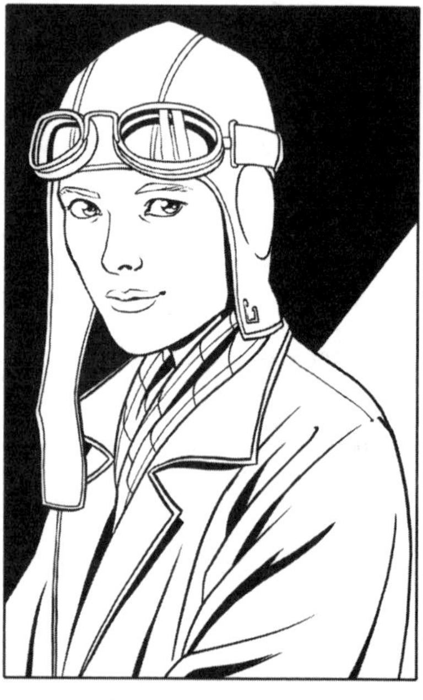

Other records soon followed. She achieved the first women's transatlantic flight, then the first solo women's transatlantic flight. Amelia soon became a national celebrity, but what really made her happy was proving that men and women were equal in "jobs requiring intelligence, coordination, speed, coolness and willpower."

Amelia kept racking up records, including the first solo flight across the Pacific from Hawaii to California. As she approached her 40th birthday in 1937, Amelia planned one last great challenge: to be the first woman to fly around the world, a distance of 29,000 miles. She departed on June 1st, and on June 29th, Amelia landed in New Guinea with only 7,000 miles to go.

Overcast skies made navigation difficult, and Amelia's radio broadcasts were often drowned out by static. At 8:45 a.m. on July 3rd, after a final radio broadcast announced that she was "running north and south", nothing was ever heard from Amelia Earhart again. In a letter she left for her husband in case anything happened on the flight, she wrote, "Please know I am quite aware of the hazards. I want to do it because I want to do it. Women must try to do things as men have tried. When they fail, their failure must be but a challenge to others."

LUCY ROBBINS WELLES LIBRARY

3 2510 11480 1830

DISCARDED

Lucy Robbins Welles Library
95 Cedar Street
Newington, CT 06111-2645